Ten Women Who Shook the World

TEN WOMEN WHO SHOOK THE WORLD

SYLVIA BROWNRIGG

VICTOR GOLLANCZ

LONDON

First published in Great Britain 1997
by Victor Gollancz
An imprint of the Cassell Group
Wellington House, 125 Strand, London WC2R 0BB

A catalogue record for this book is
available from the British Library.

ISBN 0 575 06490 0

Typeset by CentraCet, Cambridge
Printed and bound in Great Britain by
St Edmundsbury Press Ltd, Bury St Edmunds, Suffolk

97 98 99   5 4 3 2 1

Behind each of these stories is
a friend. They were written for:

El, Blake, Cathy, Jane, Lisa, Olivia, Pam T,
Pam D, Maia, and Jessica.

The collection is for them, and for all the other
earth-shaking women I know.

Contents

'I'm too tall to be a girl, I never had enough dresses to be a lady and I wouldn't call myself a woman. I'm somewhere between a chick and a broad.'

Julia Roberts

Amazon

Actually, it wasn't that hard. When they see it people say, Gosh, that must have taken her *for ever*. I want to tell them – Really, it was easier than it looks. Especially with my assistant helping. She's invaluable. I couldn't have done it without her.

The pyramids themselves went up in about three days. And that was with coffee breaks, siestas, time to talk on the phone – everything. I just don't believe in this workaholic business, you know, twenty-hour work-days and all that. It's inhuman. And it's not as though it's necessary to get things done. I told my assistant – Martha – I told Martha, 'When you get tired, now, you just take a little break. There's no point in driving yourself to exhaustion. You'll get more done if you're well-rested, fresh each day.' And you see? I was right.

Took three days. We even finished before sundown on the

third day, so we could enjoy the vantage point of our new creation while there was still light. I brought up a bottle of champagne to surprise Martha, and she was good enough to pull together some tasty snacks – cocktail olives, goat's cheese, a baguette. Sitting together on that uncomfortable little point at the top, clinking champagne glasses, we surveyed our work and the hot surrounding calm of the desert. We admired the smooth edges of the great cubed triangle we were sitting on; we joked about how, even after all that workout we'd just had building them, we both got out of breath climbing up to the top. We chatted a little about what they'd be used for – Martha thought they'd be good to stage plays in, what with how dramatic and dark and, of course, voluminous they were inside. I told her it was my understanding that people were to be buried in them. This disappointed her. 'What, all this work for dead people?' she asked me, with some indignation. I tried to explain to her that it was out of our hands at this point, that our clients had the right to do whatever they wanted with them. I could see this didn't sit well with her. I understood. She's young still, doesn't fully appreciate the nature of the job, wants to be able to keep control over everything rather than realizing that at a certain point you have to let go. I remarked that probably one day they'd degenerate into mere tourist traps anyway, and this perversely seemed to cheer her up.

After that we just sat there, watching the sun sink slowly

14

to bloody the desert, each thinking our own quiet thoughts about the world. My back ached, my brain was tired. I'm not about to deny we'd been working hard. It occurred to me that there is always a melancholy dimension to creating anything: the moment when you shrug your shoulders, declare it done and turn your eyes from it to face the next thing. I tried to communicate this to Martha with the look I gave her and a sympathetic patting of her shoulder. I don't know if she got it or not. She drained her glass, took mine from me, cleared up our things and then we went back down.

Initially it was altogether jollier working on the Great Wall. You can imagine it would be. Not quite such a morbid project, first of all, and logistically just so much easier. Also there's something intrinsically comical about building a structure for defense, and I tried to help Martha see that. (We kept our voices low, of course. I'm a professional – I'd never dream of making fun of a client to his or her face.) The thing is, I said to her as we were slapping the bricks down, working pretty fast and loose with the mortar – both wearing overalls, so we didn't mind the mud flying – who is this really going to keep out, in the end? Don't you have to expect that at some point some clever guy or gal will come along and find a way over? Defense structures date fast, I told Martha a little dogmatically, because there's always some new offensive something or other just around the corner, waiting to lay waste your precious plans. Martha told me to lighten up. It was just a wall, she said. Why not build a wall? They're cute, she said. They're very impressive from the bird's-eye view. They create a nice line in the landscape.

'Line in the landscape,' I repeated. 'My, aren't we getting sophisticated.' She threw a little mud at me then so I threw some back. We got into a mudfight. It was undignified, but fun. (The texture of the wet earth clean on your cheeks is refreshing.) As I said before, I am not a big believer in keeping people nailed to the grindstone. One good, raucous mudfight, and three extra watchtowers got built later in the day – more than I was expecting us to get through.

Of course that meant that the mood was all wrong later when I tried again to broach the serious subject of walls: what they connote, how people speak of them. 'Inside walls are a much better protection than outside walls,' I suggested with caution, but Martha merely rolled her eyes. 'That's deep,' she told me with a straight face. 'I'll think about it.'

'I'm just speaking about defense – ' I said to her. 'The metaphysics of defense, you could say, or the zen of defense.' I thought I might catch her interest with the word 'zen'. People seem to find it an appealing word.

'Am I getting double time for this?' was her answer to my philosophizing. I let it go. Later on, after the project was over, I decided to take her to task about her attitude. I don't mind irreverence, I told her, and I don't mind some kidding around, but there are times when I have something to teach her and then it would be just as well if she paid attention. She'd get double time when she was supposed to get double time, but she'd only get nuggets of thought from me when I was in the mood to dispense them. It was worth paying attention. I probably came down a little harshly, but I think you have to be firm with people and not lose your authority. There was a small coolness between us for a while after that, but I would never have dreamed of letting Martha go, so I just rode it out till relations got back to normal.

The thing was, it was a slow period after that, busywork mostly. We were twiddling our thumbs waiting for something really big to sink our teeth into. Boredom doesn't do anything very positive for a working relationship – though I suppose it gave us time to share a few discreet stories about our families and childhoods – so I was relieved when the next big project came around.

It was a cathedral. House of god, you know. It made a change. Knowing what I knew about Martha – she's not exactly an atheist, but she certainly doesn't have much tolerance for the spiritual approach – I was worried she might be sullen or even go so far as to protest or refuse. How wrong I was. She chose to skim over all the iconography there and instead took pleasure in the sheer aesthetics of the piece. As she kept pointing out, it was a remarkably beautiful work we were building (I blushed modestly when she described it that way but it was true, all true) and that, she said, was compensation for everything else. She got a crick in her neck tilting her head back to construct the complicated pattern on the ceiling; she burned her hands once or twice melting lead for the windows. But she never complained – she's a tough cookie is Martha – she just sighed in awe at the jewel we were creating.

Chart, she persisted in calling it. I told her it was Chart*res*, but she never got the hang of that last little growl in the throat. I tried teaching her French so she'd feel more at home, and she did figure out how to ask for building supplies and foodstuffs. I'll give Martha credit, she's good with people. Throw her in a new environment and she learns to adapt. So she didn't have any trouble getting around the little town there, buying her apples and potatoes and gazing awestruck at the tall towers. I'd never known Martha to be so sensitive to glory before then, to be frank with you. I could see I'd misjudged her. The passion in her eyes when she stood still in that great, hollow, holy space, the scattered light of the gem-bright stained glass falling all over her – this was a passion I hadn't known my assistant to own. At that minute her smooth face took on the golden sweetness of honey; her still, full lips the pale red of persimmon. People keep themselves private when they work with you, and there were plenty of things too that Martha didn't know about me. Still, I filed that away, that impression of her nobility. If there came a time later when I was hoping to chat with Martha about something deeper than blueprints, I'd have a chance to remind her that she had the capacity for it. I've seen your face in a rapture, I'd tell her, probably smugly. Your eyes in a blessing. We'd see what smart answer she could come up with for that.

It was not a surprise that she was all go on the next one. I predicted that the moment I heard of it. Pretty pretty mausoleum for a sadly dead wife. White pure marble the color of ice floats. Who could resist such a spectacle? Who could wait to dig in? (If death had bothered her on the pyramids, it was no longer a problem. She was a little older now, a tad more contemplative. Besides, this one was personal.) We set up shop there on the riverbank and proceeded to give shape to the Mumtaz Mahal. Later to be known, through the flawed human ear, by a name that was picked up by casinos and blues singers – the Taj Mahal.

He was a sad fellow, our client. He really did miss his wife. Martha found it all very moving, and I have to admit that even I – and I'm not usually so moved by your basic human drama, being fonder of concepts and shapes, and directional pulls – found myself choking up on occasion. He'd sweep past us in his bright grief-stricken clothes, the tears running silently and constantly down his clove-brown face. 'Make the minaret poetry,' he'd insist when he could remember how to speak. His orders carried the weight of a man sunk in mourning. 'Let the pinnacles be perfect, the parapets sheer grace.' These, we were given to understand, were of course the qualities of his wife. She was the most beautiful of the earth's creations: this description was passed along too, and it made me anxious. After all, at least god is not a figure anyone recently can have claimed to *see* – not in the sense of knowing god's haircolor or the width of his nose – so building his house gives you that much more leeway. The wife, however, was someone whose beauty was known. They wouldn't let us forget about it, and it was a lot to live up to.

Martha helped me in this case, though. She outdid her duties as my assistant. Grasping in an instinctive way the bereft peace this man lived in, she was inspired to build something that gave shape to his heart. It was teamwork on the Taj Mahal, in other words – the final project had both of our marks on it. (I once looked at her as she was working, whistling away cheerfully. I don't think she noticed me, thank goodness – it would have been embarrassing if she'd seen the admiration on my face. Would have damaged that professional rapport we had built up.) We were both extremely proud in the end, if frustrated: the thanks of the emperor were muted at best. He was moved by the white palace, and he repaid us handsomely. But we left him with shoulders sagging as sad as the first day. It would have been nice if he could have forced out just one little smile as we parted.

You get used to these slights, though. They toughen you. You knock yourself out on behalf of another person; they thank you, pay you, and send you on your way. You have to take pride in your own accomplishment and not expect profound gratitude from them because you probably won't get it. It's why you and your co-worker are there to provide each other with encouragement and praise. I mentioned this to Martha, that this was why I was a little more cynical than she was, why I didn't get so involved in clients' lives. I warned her not to get so caught up that she'd leave disappointed. There was no eye-rolling this time. She nodded, said she could see what I meant. Her sea-colored eyes frothed comprehension. Still, she said she liked to have that emotional connection with her work.

After all that drama it was good to come back to earth. As I said before, I'm fond of projects that pose questions or problems. How do you join up the Eastmost of Europe with the Eastmost of Asia? What does it really mean to connect? I got very excited by the Trans-Siberian Railway. I thought it a terrific idea and was so glad to be of help. I could tell Martha was bored, and beginning to want to strike out on her own. She wasn't getting the bigger picture. I tried to draw it for her – in the air, I mean, in her mind – I tried to tell her about opportunity and export, new settlements, migration. It wasn't like she was a stranger to travel and couldn't identify with movement. But all Martha saw when I tried to get her excited was the track after track that we were going to have to lay: the monotony of that task, the sheer repetitiveness of it. There was a terrifying moment when she said maybe I should go out there alone, that I clearly had the project in hand and might not need her assistance. My heart chilled then. I thought Martha might leave me. (It's so hard to find someone both smart and reliable.) But I stayed firm and, trying to keep the catch from my voice, told her I certainly did need her, that I couldn't do it without her. I think that flattered her into agreeing to come along. Once we got there and started, she got into the spirit of the thing. Martha's good that way – not stubborn about holding on to her once-firm beliefs. She could see its value, its lyricism even. She came to appreciate the geometry of it. This time when we finished, I thought some sort of vacation was called for – this time we really had been working hard – so I asked my client for an inaugural train ride all the way across. No skimping this time: we'd really deserved it. Caviar and blinis, cool pepper vodka. Speeding by tundra and small outposts of wedge-faced humanity. Talking and singing together late into the night. It was the perfect conclusion to our perfect labors. It's tricky, building the off-work relationship, but by now Martha and I knew each other well enough that I figured such intimacies were warranted.

Besides, by now, you see, I was thinking about retirement. I'd been at my job for so long, with such magnificent projects. I had a great deal to be proud of. And I could see that Martha wanted to strike out on her own. That work at the white palace. Her attention to detail. She had different interests from me, I knew, and I could tell she would make it big in her own way. She had that quality in her. Martha, I wanted to tell her, you've grown a lot since I first met you. You've got a wise streak now where you used to just have a keen organizational ability. That deep sympathy I saw in your eyes for the emperor in mourning – I see it in you all the time now, even when you're just on the phone placating some crabby client. Martha, you half-built the great Taj Mahal. Martha, I watched you while you slept on the Trans-Siberian Railway. Your dreams animated your face and your face then was beautiful.

I didn't tell her any of that, of course. It wouldn't exactly have been professional! Instead I let her know, quite formally, that my last project would be this upcoming bridge we were working on. She was surprised. Not so much about the retirement, but that the last one should be such a low-key, comparatively straight forward affair – building a bridge between two low hills, over a none-too-wide strip of bay. 'No, this isn't a tough one, Martha,' I confirmed to her questioning glance. 'Nonetheless, it's the one for which they'll remember me.' She shrugged, mostly to humor me, and sat back to let me give my imagination free rein.

If I'd had my way, it really *would* have been gold. I pictured a great, golden gateway into that spectacular mountain-hugged bay. Maybe I was getting old, a little whimsical, a little crazy. In the old days of course I was very simple with materials – brick, mortar and mud were all that I needed. Maybe it was the railroad ties that gave me this urge towards metal. Maybe the time had finally come when I wanted to show off. Needless to say, the gold plan was shot down – I guess I didn't have the influence I'd have had some years earlier. My genius was questionable these days. What could I do? We painted it orange instead. Martha consoled me about this last lost battle. She said the color would look lovely. She also pointed out, under her breath – Martha had gained tact, over the years – that they were just going to have to go on painting that bridge, year after year, to keep it the characteristic orange. It would become a tourist landmark, she predicted, just like the pyramids. There would come a day, forty years into repainting, when they'd regret not having just built the whole darn thing out of gold like I'd wanted to.

Golden Gate Bridge. Don't know whether you've seen it. If I were to pick a swan song – I mean, thousands of years ago, when I was there in the desert with Martha in the early days, if you'd asked me to pick a swan song then – I wonder if I could have closed my eyes and imagined it. Something gloriously transitional, perhaps I'd have said – some great landmark of hope, something forward-looking, something new worldish. A piece that speaks to freedom and travel – to movement, and balance, and grace over water.

I have time to get philosophical about these things now I've retired. I bore Martha with my speculations, my memories. She lets me. She's indulgent. Half the time she probably isn't even listening. That's all right. She's busy, I know. Deadlines of her own to meet.

24

It's pleasant here in the jungle – certainly different from the kinds of community folks normally retire to. Very green and steamy, lots of animals and birds. I've never been that compelled by wildlife, but Martha's helped me to hear the joy in a parrot cry, to admire the flicker of snakes in the grass. We're here because of her. This is her project. You can't say the girl's not ambitious. Landscape gardening I call it, when I want to bug her. It's not true – it's just my joke. She's actually redesigning and fixing up the rainforest, that's what she's doing. It's been so wrecked by everybody. They needed someone with a lot of energy – and that's my Martha, all right – to come along and try to pull it back together. So she's in there day after day, replanting and reseeding, drawing up new plans; stripping out the man-made garbage and trying to restore the place to some of its former magnificence.

I admire her. It's nothing I would have done. This is a new generation, right? You've got to expect their priorities to be different. It doesn't bother me one bit. I know Martha admires me and the work I've done. She's old enough now to admit that she learned a lot from me, all through those years when she was my assistant. Graciousness is something that's come to her as she's matured.

Besides, how can I begrudge her this? You remember that rapturous look I mentioned way back in Chartres? (Or '*Chart*' – I still tease her sometimes about that.) That expression is on her face nearly every evening now, when she returns from a

25

full day's work in the forest. She comes back to me, her eyes bright and holy, and she lets me chatter on for a while with my reminiscences, my small revelations. I lay back with my head on the moist alive ground, staring right up at her pretty face, and she's kind enough to draw her hands through my hair, soothing me as I reconstruct my past. Later, after we've dined, we switch roles. I'll sit up with Martha's delicate strong frame in front of me and I'll rub some relaxation into her warm neck and shoulders. So tight, after all her work for the day. Out of her mouth will spill stories of the riverlife and the forest, the trees she's nursing back into existence, the hope she has for the tigers and tapirs, the monkeys and mongeese, the many small toads. She speaks of the rubber plants that will no longer be bled to make superballs, she chats about the wood that will never again become A-frames. She talks of tearing down factories. She revels in getting rid of the office sprawl.

Martha tells me of her day's work unbuilding. Graceful, calm, sure of herself now. While she tells me about her hopes for the future the sun abandons our forest to its jungly darkness. I hold her shoulders in my fading fingers, touching her carefully, knowing with pride that she will realize them all.

A Gal of Ambition

When he died, I wasn't sure who to call. I thought of Brian – Brian would have wanted to know. He's interested in that kind of thing. But I haven't felt the same about Brian since the dog incident, so I thought I'd skip it, let him find out for himself. I'm not here to be a dispenser of information.

I did call Phyllis. Phyllis has a good ear for troubles. It's because she has so many herself. You're hardly started on your situation when Phyllis says, 'I know just what you mean!' and proceeds to tell you a story which is, as it turns out, uncannily like your own. I think Phyllis has lived a hundred lives: no matter what's happened, she'll come up with a catastrophe to match anyone's. The only thing I've told her that ever really floored her was the story about me and Brian and the dog. That took her breath away. 'It's shocking,' she managed finally, which is pretty minimal for Phyllis. Usually she delivers whole paragraphs. 'I know,' I said then. 'It shocked me.'

So all I had to say this time was, 'He seemed a gentle man,' and Phyllis was off.

'Death!' she started, grandly. 'What I don't know about death!'

'I know,' I said.

'Was it peaceful?' she asked. Her choice of story depended on the answer.

'I'm not sure,' I told her. 'I asked the ambulance man that same question, but he was too busy making sure his gloves were on tight to answer me.'

'Probably not.'

'What?'

'I mean, it probably wasn't peaceful. They usually aren't. Unless the person is chock full of drugs, but that's another story. Then they go out like a zombie, and no one has the chance to say that last goodbye, and the person themself can't muster up any last words, the way they always do in the movies.'

'He probably did have drugs. After all, they say that's how he—'

'Though of course these days most people don't need last words, they've already taped or videoed themselves in some better-looking moment, so when it comes time for "last words" all you've got to do is press *play* and you get the whole thing, pre-recorded. Which *is* sort of like the movies, if you think about it.'

'He didn't have a VCR,' I told her. 'He used to ask to borrow mine.'

'Did you let him?'

'No.'

'That's smart. You'd never see it again, especially if he was into drugs. ——But it doesn't have to be a video. A tape recorder'll do it. Have I ever told you the story of my friend Frieda?' She'd finally found it: she'd finally found the matching story.

'No.'

'She was diagnosed with something – Redgrave's Disease, I think they called it. One of those terrible things where one week you're twitching, the next you can't move your leg, and finally you're eating pizza through a straw and trying to communicate using your eyebrows.'

'I've never heard of it.'

'Well, who can keep up with all the diseases they keep discovering? I used to write them down on index cards and try to keep them all alphabetized, but I couldn't keep up. Anyway, Henry said it was morbid and he threw them out. And what page does Henry turn to every morning, right after headlines and sports scores? Obituaries. But *I'm* too morbid.'

'I don't like obituaries. They're repetitive. They don't give you a real sense of the person.'

'Anyway, Frieda gets diagnosed with Redgrave's Disease, and the only people she tells are me and the guy who's always fixing her typewriter. Frieda's one of the only people I know with a typewriter, and there's about three people left in the world who know how to fix them. And one of them is her friend, the guy she tells about having Redgrave's.'

'What is she, a writer?'

'Was,' Phyllis corrected me. 'She *was* someone who had a lot of correspondence with people who lived abroad. She didn't like to talk about it. She wasn't married. But, as far as I knew, that was all she wrote. She was a telephone operator by profession.'

'You think she was after the guy who fixed her typewriter?'

'No, no! I'll tell you. She wasn't. But she needed someone to confide in – someone who could help her. Besides, the typewriter guy was married.'

'That never stops people.'

'You didn't know Frieda,' Phyllis said sharply. I was cutting in too much. '*Anyway*, she goes down to this guy's little shop, tells him her troubles, and says she figures she has about a month to live – that's what the doctor told her – and she needs his help. She says she wants to borrow some tape recorder equipment. She tells him it's to record a message for her friends and family, not that she has much family, just a

32

sister who lives a thousand miles away who she hasn't spoken to in seven years.'

'Why can't she just type her message – if the machine is working?'

'Because she's got Redgrave's and is rapidly losing sensation in her extremities!' Phyllis barked. 'It would have started out "to my dear friends" and then in a day or two all she'd be able to type is "fffff". —She has to tape it. So the guy says he'll help her, he'll come over to her apartment and tape her message for her.'

'You see what I mean? So what happens – he makes a pass at her?'

'Certainly not. He comes over, records her message, and then packages it up for her in a nice little box, a black box, that he made himself. He writes "Last Words by Miss Frieda Martin" on the box, trying to fake her handwriting so it doesn't look like he interfered.'

'And then on the tape it turns out she leaves all her worldly possessions to Mr Typewriter.'

Phyllis breezed right past me. 'The other thing he did for her was something she had asked him that was a little more difficult. She asked him to bring her some drugs. Because Frieda – and who can blame her? – wanted to go quiet, peaceful, none of this shuddering and wreckage business. And she did *not* want to wind up eating her pizza through a straw.'

'Why didn't she ask you—?'

'I don't know, but she didn't. She asked him. She wanted *his* help. Maybe she thought I'd be – indiscreet.' Phyllis paused. 'Though I wouldn't have been. I wouldn't have told a soul.' She coughed. 'So the same day he taped her message, he brought over all the drugs he could get, a funny mixture of Valium and antihistamines and codeine and some mysterious little pellets he'd never finished from when he had a terrible case of poison oak. He also brought over a bottle of whiskey, in case that would help, and then just to be really safe he threw in some cleaning product that was supposed to be "dangerous if swallowed."'

'Jeez! What was he trying to do – kill her?'

'He was trying to *help*,' Phyllis said. Then she was quiet for a second. She always stages at least one strategic silence. 'So do you want to hear what the tape said?'

'Well, what happened to Frieda? She died?'

'Of course she did. She died that night. Cardiac arrest induced by narcotics.'

'And no one arrested Mr Typewriter?'

'How could they? All they knew was that someone had given her some strange drugs to help her kill herself. He threw out all the containers, of course. He was a careful man. And no one knew that they knew each other. Your typewriter repairman generally doesn't come up for questioning in a case like that.'

'How did you find out about him?'

'Oh, he had to confess to someone, so finally, two months later, he called me up and told me. *I* didn't care. I thought the whole thing was perfectly reasonable.' She paused. 'Listen, do you want to hear what the tape said or not, because I've got to be quick. My soap comes on in five minutes.'

I still hadn't told her, not really, about my upstairs neighbor: what he was like, his bright taste in house plants, the time he told me about his mother's work with orphaned babies in some remote part of town. I hadn't even said what he died of. It was AIDS. I'd been wondering if Phyllis had any AIDS stories, which might have been interesting. But she was way too far into this tape business to stop now, so I told her to tell me. The AIDS could wait, I decided.

'Well, there were only three of us at the tape-reading. I'll have to skip how I found the black box and the tape, and how I realized what it was, and how I cried at the window of Frieda's tiny apartment thinking about the things people go through to try to communicate.' She coughed again. 'I tried to think who should hear these last words with me, and finally I just picked me and two of her downstairs neighbors. They were the only ones I could think of who knew her. Besides, what if the tape was a little – you know -- *strange?* They say with Redgrave's you begin to lose your mind. —But what it was, finally, Frieda's "last words"? – well, they didn't even specify anything about her things or who was to be left with what (not that there was a lot in the place, it was the size of a shoebox); they just started with, "For the past ten years I've been working on a novel. The first ten chapters are in my middle desk drawer. It's the story of a woman, spurned at an early age, who sets out on a life of prayer and adventure, though no one realizes this about her as she's just a telephone operator . . ." and it goes on and on, and tells the *whole story*, as she's mapped it out, of this novel.'

'And is it good? Is it interesting?'

'Is it *good*? That's not the point! The point is that there wasn't anything else on that whole tape, which we sat there listening to for an hour and a half! And do you know what it ends with?'

'What?'

'And then I really have to go. It ends – her last sentence, after finishing the novel's story line, is just this: "I leave this for you because I believe someone should finish the novel I've begun. It won't be too hard to imitate my style, and it's a story that must be told."'

Now I was silenced. I couldn't even say, 'It's shocking,' because it wasn't, exactly. It was just – strange. A little spooky.

'Are you still there?' Phyllis asked. 'Because I've got to go.'

'But, wait – what happened to the tapes?'

'Oh, I have them,' she said casually. 'And the chapters. I mean, I couldn't throw them away, could I? When I die, someone else can decide what to do with them. Unless you know any budding novelists who want to write about a woman spurned.'

'Well . . .' I said doubtfully. I have to admit I thought of Brian.

'Ooops – the credits are rolling! I'll talk to you later, hon. Sorry to hear about the neighbor. But think of it this way – if he was a druggie, at least he probably went peaceful. Plus sooner or later he would have died anyway, of an overdose. Bye!'

I thanked her and said goodbye.

Her strange story had set wheels going in my head. This one was better than usual for Phyllis, I had to admit: more complicated, and with an open-endedness to it that I liked.

I thought of Brian, the artist, the writer, the creative man. He's the only person I really know who's that way, and he's it *all the way* – he's always ready to perform for a crowd, to dance in a musical, to write poems on some abandoned wall. Brian, I knew, would really go to town with ten chapters of a novel about a woman spurned. He'd probably really turn it into something. 'A life of prayer and adventure,' as Phyllis said. He could make it poetry, I bet.

I remembered what I'd thought that morning, as the ambulance men came to clear away my neighbor's poor emaciated body. (I hoped to God he did have drugs – it looked more like he'd starved to death.) As I watched the hopeless spinning light on top of the van, I thought about calling Brian and telling him. He's always interested in the human drama – always looking for material, he says.

But then I thought about that poor dead dog, and what he did with it – 'in the name of art,' he promised me. It was unforgivable. I can't stand cruelty to animals. Even dead ones.

Hussie from the West

I lasso, I corral, I ride 'em, they buck.

But not too often, they don't. I've got pretty good control.

You know, it depends where you are, what it is. Bulls, horses; men, women; — ideas. I take pretty much the same approach, whatever it is. Hold on to 'em as long as possible, even if they're bucking, because the longer you ride, the more of the soul of the thing makes it into your own body: the more you and the thing become one, become *it*. At least for a while.

I've been called promiscuous. Not a pretty word, is it? Makes you think of the gloop that comes out of your nose or what comes up your throat when you're gagging, if you're trying to swallow down something you didn't necessarily mean to swallow. *Promiscuous*: your face has to pucker when you say it.

I prefer to think of myself as an adventurer. Charting the souls of so many of god's creatures, and of the floaty beings that populate the land of notions. It's a job. It's a calling. It takes strong thigh muscles, intelligence, cunning, a good pair of boots. It takes heart, in fact. The heart to stay on. To not be defeated. The heart to move the blood to keep the fingers spry to keep the skin tight to keep the eyes wide and open and ready always, still, not just to see what the world looks like from on board but to take in the mountains that surround you, the pure air, that great sky that changes and stays the same, the sky we only really have in the West.

I remember a she-bull I rode once. She was spiteful and red-tongued, with close black hair and narrowing eyes. A brutal hoof. Musty breath. But her muscles between my legs were smooth and ripply like a cool stream for trout, or the best kind of ice cream. There was a thrill there. I gripped and stayed while she tried hard to lose me, and in those few seconds we had together I had the illusion of understanding the life of the bull, sympathizing even with its bottled frustration and its sinewy fury. Caged and taunted it lived its should-have-been grand life, suffering the prods and brands – real and imagined – of a crowdful of strange-hatted strangers. It was humiliating, I realized. Having nowhere to go with all that passion. Just as I understood this, though, she tossed me into the sky for a long, full minute, sent me tumbling through the cloudy air that's thin on oxygen and pushes a mind to the

42

brink of hallucination. As I tumbled, I dreamed: a world of bulls, each with its one mean secret, its tiny kernel of truth, letting me on for my brief exploration, my quick lust, my epiphany. Throwing me off, after, up into the clouds, dissatisfied with my technique maybe or else just hungry for a different pair of legs to grip them. Bulls carpeted the ground like grass in my dream, there was no escaping them. All dark, some horned, some snorting; all shes.

It was easier with horses.

A horse has that famous nobility lacked by a bull. With a horse you enter into a kinder agreement. You share the beginnings of a vocabulary. 'Go,' you say, click-clicking your tongue, and if the horse approves the moment and the direction, he'll do it. He'll take you. The language you speak to the horse is one of voice, hands, leather and metal; a touch here, a spike there, a 'Hold it!', a 'Whoa, boy!', a 'Gideeyap! Come on!' Chomping at his bit like someone gnashing their teeth in their sleep, the horse replies through speed and smoothness, occasionally issuing its own hoarse, ancient call in a sound of distress or indignation. The conversation, if it works, is the kind I would choose if I were free to choose any kind: about the right shape of adventure, about what it is to feel exhilarated, about whether in the end two creatures can want the same thing at the same time and then somehow satisfy that shared single desire.

I had it once on a palomino. We were riding out in

moonlight, threading blue-black oak trees as we trod the dry trail. The yellow chaparral grasses were periwinkle at that hour; the horse glowed with wisdom; and me, I was blue-jeaned and bare-chested, resting my brown boots against the horse's flank but not kicking, because I didn't yet want to force the pace. No sound but the shuffling drumbeat of hooves on the path. The sweet smell of midnight weeds and hidden wildflowers. Western stars crooning their cowboy melody down over us as we moved towards the place we were going to.

When the horse started trotting, I was ready, and though I wanted to see this precious landscape around us I leaned in, leaned down, and pressed my downed cheek against the warm fur of the horse's neck. I closed my eyes. At this moment, I was trusting. I believed the horse would find the way. I allowed that the horse, though stronger and better than me, had an intuition about my wordless needs and would not endanger me. The trot became a dance, a polka. The trot took us to a charming place, where I was charmed. Then, half-asleep, not in this world but in the world of our joint movement, I responded to an urgency from my body. I kicked the horse a little – just an edge of a heel, just an encouragement – not a threat but a promise. It worked. The horse galloped.

And it is hard to keep your poise when galloping, it's hard to be elegant then. My hair was flying. My legs bounced. My breasts may have jumped. In any case elegance is being untouchable and I was touched, I was moved then and if I shouted into the night's silence it was only further proof that the call of a good ride is not like other calls, it comes from your gut and takes no form of words and may rupture silences, even those silences you had intended to keep.

That was a good ride.

Though I didn't even know the horse, and never took him out again. I do remember the cooling sweat in his hot mane, my fingers through that coarse hair. I remember saying, 'Sweet boy,' to him as we slowed back down, my only shaped words of that deep evening.

With men the ride is not always so free. With men there is the cost incurred by speaking one and not the same tongue. 'Let's go!' he says, and you say, 'Sure! Where to?' and he says, 'Oh. I thought you knew.' A sourness curls his mouth down to a sulk. 'I am your friend,' you say to him, and he says, 'And I am yours,' and you look at each other with suspicion, wondering how the other could be both so bold and so absurd. He opens a wallet stocked with money and free passes, the card of someone he met on the airplane, a reference he's been meaning to look up. You peer into the battered leather pouch looking for photobooth snaps of friends, or ticket stubs; a lock of hair, a comb, a diamond. What is it exactly he keeps in there and what is he missing? If you rode a train together right now, ran alongside it and hopped on the way they do in movies, would he have enough stories to last you till you got to the final destination? What would the clattering-by countryside provoke in him? Would he lay you down on the thin hay of the cool compartment and then in that locomotive rhythm would you finally find a way to love and to read each other? Maybe so. Maybe it would be on the cold, hard, shifting surface that you'd come to recognize the face behind the eyes, the heart behind the gesture. It's hard to know, isn't it? It's hard to say. With a man, I've found, it's hard to say.

With a woman you could say so much that sometimes the temptation is not to speak at all. In a small white room with a woman you might look at each other and think, 'Yes,' and that would be the only word required and even then it would seem a shame to say it because there can be so much tension in the not saying, there can be that quiet want and comprehension when no one says anything and it's just touched palms that light the blaze. This happens between women. Between two women with blonde hair stepping down a street and pressing shoulders; between a light-haired woman and a dark-haired sipping hot milk together late at night in the pretense that they are trying to get to sleep; between two dark-haired women in a smoky bar, when finally the drink makes no difference because the fantasy's there without the drink and more bottles just mean more glass to knock down on the way to consummation.

Then too it can go the other way with women. They are

your enemies. They'll eat you alive. You might wake up in the morning to find your own tongue utterly unraveled, leaving you unable even to tell the story of how you got here or to ask the body lying next to you why she did it. You might fly apart from the force pulling you outwards. Your guts might reverse their action in the course of confusion, of being uncertain any longer which way is up and which way gravity was supposed to pull you. With a woman you could open your mouth and hear a stranger's voice come out of it, speaking in new slang with unfamiliar witticisms. 'Let's go for a ride,' you might say to a woman, meaning a television commercial on an open road with the top down. What she'd give you is six hours in the desert in a sweaty, dark, claustrophobic army tank. What she'd give you is a packed mini-van full of bored youngsters demanding more candy and throwing up in the back seat. What she'd give you is a motorcycle spin across the bridge, the Pacific out to port and the Bay to starboard, your face orange in the reflected light of the paint, your nose and throat full of that clean sunlight, the wind cutting into your teeth as the bit did the horse's.

You never know who's riding who, with a woman, and that's the one thing that makes the experience worth the care and fear, the bliss and misery. You think it's your hand reining her in, saying, 'No, no, slow down,' when you feel her strong arm around your waist pulling you back from a brink of your own. You kick her to go faster and she reminds you that you've already arrived and the journey's over; that you are sleeping now in the bed and dreaming of another afternoon. You have the sensation of being in control when suddenly you feel those knees around your ears and the pressure all down your back and you realize you've no choice, none, but to keep running and running, with her on top of you, to hope you hear her pleasure calling down to you, and not to admit that you're tired, not to slow or to stop till she gets where she wants, till she reaches down and pets your cheek and says, 'Good girl. That's it. Good girl.'

If you're fed up or bitter, it's simple: you buck. One powerful jolt of the haunches, one heart-thrust, one rejection. Anyone can do it. The plain, tough absolute of *no*. And she's gone. And it's over. And the love ends, the ride is up, the carousel slows, the ponies stop dipping and rising. The world stops spinning and you get off and back into it, your vocabulary restored, your hair settling back down again, still breathing the last moments of exhilaration as your pink cheeks suggest to others your previous enjoyment.

An idea is your most faithful friend. Sometimes I feel this. Am I promiscuous, or an adventurer? If I am promiscuous then each of those creatures I've mentioned is too because as I've ridden them they've ridden me and I am not the one who has called all those shots. If I am promiscuous then so is that bed I slept in where nothing happened but the hope of love; and so is that train compartment where our eyes met; and so

is my favorite novel that has dozed beside me over the years
in times of trouble or confusion when I've needed its solace;
and so are the ideas I've corralled, some briefly, some longer,
the ideas of romance and disappointment and language and the
West.

Like a blanket, the idea of the West has thrown itself
around me, warming my shoulders with homesickness and
reminding me of that chilly summer night air which so often
contains the scent of forgotten flowers. Like a pillow, the idea
of the West has cradled my head for colorful dreams, like the
dream of a blonde-maned actress and the dream of a runaway
train, on fire; the dream of turquoise-bright fish jumping in a
cold clear stream and the one of great, gold hillsides spiced by
the green spears of eucalyptus. Like a bed, the idea of the
West's where I'll start and finish, where each night I'll go for
my renewal, and which each morning I'll leave in that daily
botched effort to inhabit my present geography.

They say once you learn to ride the idea of the West, you
never forget it. If you're born there you learn it early, in
those first confusing years when you're making the effort to
place yourself, to carve out the I, to memorize the names
given to streets and the place your vast state has in the broader
scheme of things. Without knowing it, you learn to pedal
yourself along the idea of wide roads and open skies, the
concept of land not yet fenced off, the notion that even when
you are happiest in the wild world a rattlesnake may come

along to bite you to oblivion. Before you're tall or ten you have cruised a highway of sun and gold and privilege. In your mind you admit the forgotten, repressed history, the people who once were, the people we tamed. On a silent dark night you approach the sleepy mares in the nearby stable, you take one out, you find a hillside path. 'This is mine, all mine,' you say to the mare on the walk. Though you're a little girl you have understood the fantasy that is the West. The freedom to own and to travel. The freedom to imagine yourself all alone.

It's in the West that I learned to be adventurous. What can I say? I've known how to do it since I've been old enough to speak. We wouldn't have legs, would we, if we weren't meant to ride? We wouldn't have hands, or voice, or the ability to grip, or the ability to make distinctions, to choose and to comprehend. Why have these talents and not use them? Why let love atrophy like a dead muscle?

In the West they understand these things. That's why at night, if there's no one else beside me, that's where I go. To breathe. To move. To plot my next adventure.

In the West, the other creatures want to go with you, and they are filled with glory, not blame. They, too, are eager to take a small bite of your soul.

The Bird Chick

At first we thought all she did was feed them. You know, there's one in every town. Some lady with ruffled coats puffing her up, her gray hair tangled, a little arm diving deep into a crumb-lined plastic bag and then flinging them, bread-bits, at her sweet babies -- the tattered brown ducks that greet her with greedy dark eyes and a flap-splattering of wings.

We thought she was one of those.

It was only later that we found out she'd been talking to them all along.

Admittedly, she was classier from the start than the other folks in that category. Younger, too. This was the 1960s, remember, when youth culture was everywhere and fashions went wild. A typical outfit for her – and she stood out in our park wearing this, to give you an idea of the plain sort of park that it was – consisted of thigh-high white boots and a brief purple miniskirt, a fluffy fake fur coat striped in skunk colors. She looked terrific in that outfit, to tell you the truth. People would have certainly noticed her and tried to talk to her, if she hadn't been so busy feeding the birds.

The fact is, most people get in the habit of ignoring people like that. That's just how it is in parks, which are controlled environments, of course, but never so controlled that you don't have to make your own decisions about who to avoid. I should know. I was going to the park quite regularly myself at that time, strolling along with my little ones, and I had to figure out for myself who made it into the 'hello' camp and who definitely didn't. Included on the yes-list were the clown man who protested about the eating of red meat (I thought he had a point, though vegetarianism still seemed kinky to me then); the nice pair of mothers who spoke in a brittle language from a cold country but who smiled so peaceably; the blue-suited policeman, who seemed always to daydream and was an unlikely crimestopper; and the long-haired young boys who in those days still kicked a football around, having not yet jellied their limbs with video games and drugs.

Not included on the hello list were the sinister characters who lurked behind trees. Sometimes you saw them or heard them, other times you just knew they were there. One was a blank white man who proclaimed with hungry pleasure about the end of the world. Another was a yo-yo obsessive, who always seemed on the brink of nervous collapse. Then there were those mysterious little children who appeared to be parentless – I knew I should take pity on them and give them chocolate or raisins but I couldn't bring myself to do it. Another in this sad, greetingless category, though it shames me now to say it, was the bird chick herself, that tall slender gal who spent her hours with flying things.

She had theatrical ambitions. This was how I later reconstructed her story – well, with the help of the magazine articles and documentaries about her that came later. She came from a family of dancers and declaimers, so she always had a sense of the value of spectacle. She'd once tried her hand at the path of convention – a month in the drama school, training how to bray like a donkey – before she realized that she had to cut loose from all that, that her style of performance could not be caged in in that way.

She set out for the park, where she felt there were still opportunities. Park performance was an undercanvassed medium, she felt, and as you know in this she was just ahead of the be-ins and happenings. In the park she saw a universe of potential audience, a small sampling of the cosmos: babies and mothers, couples, loners and dogs. Foreigners and locals. Teams gathered for unspecified sports. All of these she could speak to, she felt, once she had discovered the right dramatic language.

So while the rest of us wove our checkerboard paths

through that great green and treed park, going through our routines, the bird chick made her home by the gray pond, developing her company.

That is, she talked to the birds.

She told them, in a bird dialect not known by many, that she needed them for her project. She explained to the ducks and the swans that they had unexplored talents. She flattered them, the way people do when they want something from others. She cooed over the swans' long necks, the purity of their oh-so-white feathers. She admired the colors on the teal ducks, claimed they were eye-catching and unusual. She applauded aloud, actually – she would have drawn stares except that in that environment, as I've mentioned, people chose rather to avoid trouble and look away – when some of the little mergansers bobbed their heads beneath the water, leaving their pointed behinds fluffing comically straight up. She acted as if she'd never seen that before – laughing riotously each time they did it. She sighed with exaggerated pleasure at the deep call-chirps of widgeons. And, of course, when the geese took flight, she couldn't say enough about her awe at their technique, the grace and originality of their pattern, the fluid way that they flew together, flapping in unison, while yet retaining the strength of their individual selves. She particularly admired that, she said, and felt that it would come in handy in what she wanted them all to work towards. Because a theatrical production – she chose the sporting metaphor rather than the domestic one, because her own family was troubled and scattered and couldn't really provide a good role model for the birds – was like playing on a team. Everyone was important for their separate contributions; everyone had their moment to be appreciated for their particular talent. Like that occasion towards the end of a pop concert when the lead singer goes around and introduces the band, the bird chick promised each member of the troupe their chance in the spotlight, their time of recognition. At the same time – and she emphasized this point, because as she said she wouldn't get anywhere with a gaggle of primadonnas – everyone had to realize that *all* the contributions were important, and acknowledge the significance of everyone else's work. The thing fell apart if they didn't all work together. From the person who helped move props on stage to whoever was chosen to give the big, set speeches, everyone had a part to play, quite literally, in the great production. She didn't want to see any sulking or competitiveness. It was a team work, a love-in, a collective effort. It was perfect harmony, it was the real thing.

The birds bought it.

Who can blame them? Some say the birds were a little naïve in this all along, but I say, when you have a person with the charisma it was later clear that she had, leading you on to an unforeseen future – the chances are you'll agree to anything. Inspired by her confidence in you you'll place all your confidence in her; drawn in by her promises of all you can accomplish you'll promise her yet more, you'll lay your neck on the line for her, you'll give her your all. This is the great thing about leadership: with it you get people doing what they never thought they could. It should hardly be surprising that a few feathers get ruffled along the way.

Shakespeare in the Park, that was her ambition. By the time the spring hit that year, the rest of us – how very ordinary we'd started to look, you know, in our middle-length dresses and our plain pink makeup! How boring we'd started to feel next to this surge of creativity – we were beginning to catch on. You couldn't tell at first what was taking place out there, but out of the corner of your eye, that eye you used to turn away from her because you'd labeled her a crazy, you did start to notice some strange behavior among the waterfowl. They seemed to swim more in formation. They held their heads higher. When children proffered stale breadcrusts there was less feverish gratitude. The bird chick, in rehearsing them, had encouraged in them the beginnings of self-respect, which was bound to alter the way they dealt with everyone else in the park.

For the longest time we couldn't tell what was happening. It did seem that there was a lot of communication going on, and at certain times of the day – dawn and dusk mostly, when the park was all but empty – a flurry of activity jumbled its corners. As the reporting later made clear, they were practicing scenes then. I know it's hard to imagine how any of us could have been unaware of what was going on, but I'm trying to convey to you what it's like when you're first in the presence of something so new, something your thoughts don't yet have a name for. It was the 60s, of course, and that kept happening then: someone would come along with an idea that seemed so utterly astounding that when you first heard it, it sounded like gibberish. The moonwalk, the Xerox machine, swear words in poetry, long hair on the Beatles. All of it took some getting used to. Any of those things, the first time you heard about them, seemed highly unlikely. You can't totally blame us if what we heard first of all there were honkings and quacks.

It wasn't until the bird chick started publicizing that the buzz really started in among those of us who used the park regularly. The air sparked with curiosity, the mothers altered their gossip. Gone was the small chit-chat about walking developments and the best brand of cereal; instead when we saw each other we whispered, as if it were illegal or subversive, about the pink pamphlets we'd seen here and there. Shakespeare in the Park, they simply suggested, with Native Performers. Women's toilets, men's, teahouses, benches: the pamphlets were scattered around where they'd catch your eye, and written with enough vagueness that they nabbed your attention. We became eager to know what precisely was meant by the word 'native.' (Still people hadn't made the imaginative leap that would later seem obvious.) Even the people you'd normally avoid seemed worth talking to about the mystery. The yo-yoer stopped yo-yoing for the sake of discussion. I bribed small children with candies to find out what they'd heard. The religious preacher was struck mute by the mention of Shakespeare.

When the performances started they changed everything forever. That first evening, I'll never forget it. People had come from far and wide – I mean, including people who'd never set foot in the park before, people who barely understood what a park really was – to see this latest event. I guess the word had gotten round that there was something new in the park here, so even with the word 'Shakespeare' attached it seemed daring, near revolutionary. It might have been the word 'native' that got the long-haired people out. In those days there was a swell of interest in the oppression of such groups. T-shirts sporting political figures (Mao, Che Guevara) were visible in the crowd. Round Lennon glasses on faces blank but committed. Blonde-haired chicks, skinny and miniskirted, who could have been clones of the bird chick herself. As I say, this wasn't our usual crowd in the park – most of us were so normal in our dress and beliefs. I know some of the other park-goers felt we'd been invaded and were resentful. For myself, I had the opposite reaction: I suddenly felt very self-conscious that I'd yet to make a contribution to the burgeoning counter-culture. My first daring act was to attend this performance.

It was *Hamlet*. Ambitious, I know. The bird chick didn't do things by halves. An easier choice would have been one of the comedies, or else a history that people didn't have too much invested in – *Julius Caesar*, say, one that people were already used to seeing in modern dress and the like. But the bird chick and company went straight for the jugular. 'To be or not to be' and 'Good night, sweet prince,' the lines everyone has an opinion on, a feeling for, the lines that everyone thrills to.

For that very reason it was in fact a good choice, because the lines were delivered in that bird dialect understood by so few. Since it was *Hamlet* the thing was quite followable. You understood that the white swan was Hamlet, shuddering with grief, self-doubt and intelligence; that a widgeon was Claudius, praying for redemption all too guiltily; a bright teal was Ophelia, drowning in loveliness. If the finer points of the Yorick speech were missed, the sheer bluntness of our mortality there was not: you felt a sober shiver pass through the audience as Hamlet remembered his old buddy and spoke poems over his skull. Very little, you may be surprised to hear, failed to come across in the bird chick company's version. There were times I even thought I heard the bird equivalent of the sharper phrases I waited for – 'honeying and making love over the nasty sty', for example, or ''Tis an unweeded garden, that grows to seed; things rank and gross in nature possess it merely.' In the interval chatter I gathered that for some the blurred meanings made the play all the more poignant: they understood the broad honk and sweep of Hamlet's progression, while not being distracted by individual words. There was also something that struck at the hearts of the more politically minded, at seeing this most famous drama of great literature acted out by the dispossessed. This was one of those points that was bound to pass by an ordinary viewer like me. Though I can affirm that it was strangely stirring to hear the rhythms of the bard – even in translation – come out of the beak of a snow-feathered swan.

The rest of the story has become so famous that I feel my own contribution may as well end soon. What I thought might interest is an account by someone like me who knew the original environment that the scheme was first hatched in. Also someone who could testify without bias as to the effect on the birds. Because from where I sat that first night, those birds seemed to me to be uplifted by their performance. (As indeed we all were.) I am not any kind of poet but I can say that there was a color in their eyes that was the pride of accomplishment; that I've never seen wings beat with such purpose and glory; that, in fact, birds seemed to me that night wiser than humans, with deeper emotions and a better comprehension of the deep questions of life. That is how those birds seemed to me that night, and whatever happened later I believe what I saw was real.

Nowadays we know these stories so well, we can write them before the papers do. I'm older, I understand how it goes. In those days I was impressionable – very – and so when the bird chick rose to fast fame I thought it would last. I believed the reports that she had changed the face of theater forever; I believed the claim that she had invented a new language for drama. I appreciated the appreciation of her drawing into the center a marginalized group to perform, the description of her as a true revolutionary. (High praise in those days.) I had every reason to believe these things. After all, there was no question that she had changed *us*, the park-goers, with her work. We were all, I know, more charitable with each other after Shakespeare in the Park. More patient with each other's foibles. More tolerant of our private strangenesses and habits.

But someone was bound to come along to knock her down, once they'd gone to the trouble of setting her up. As you know, it was the charge of exploitation that did it. How nasty were those very same writers who'd so praised her at first. One month they were happily profiling the unusual stars of the play, the next throwing dim light on the so-called indignity of that casting. What had been the innovative, raw style of the bird chick became the clichéd mannerisms of one born to oppress. People who called themselves champions of the birds came in to shut the thing down, claiming ridiculous wages and non-standard treatment. (How can you expect standards, I

wondered, when the very point was to break them?) You
know all this. You remember all that fuss, or have read about
it since. You remember how the bird chick's life story went
in reverse: from admirable swan to crude ugly duckling gone
bankrupt, someone her once friendly colleagues were all too
eager to chuck from the nest.

Towards the end, when she was such a controversial figure
and I knew it might be valuable, I tried to secure the bird
chick's autograph. That sounds crasser than I mean it. It
wasn't just monetary. The bird chick and her troupe really
had changed my life. I wore short skirts these days. I had dyed
my hair brighter. I experimented with boots, and had a greater
interest in art. All of that was because of her, though her time
was waning. I wanted to touch her, if I could, to have some
souvenir of her and also to convey to her what she'd meant to
so many of us in the park.

By then she was avoiding the press. She was everything but
shattered. She was looking a little scraggly, to tell you the
truth, a little down on her luck. If I hadn't known better by
then I'd have thought her disreputable.

She sat on a bench, talking in a low voice to the birds.
From the same plastic bag she still scattered breadcrumbs –
the very non-standard treatment complained about by those
self-righteous warriors. (Where were they now? What did
they really care for birds? They were off somewhere else, no
doubt, fighting another battle that wasn't their own.) I told

my children to wait for me and I approached the bird chick
cautiously, not wanting to scare her. The autograph book
shook in my hand. I'd never actually been this close to her
before, what with avoiding her at first and then knowing she
was inaccessible once she was famous. From close to, she was
beautiful. A wrecked sternness in her features and a softness
about the eyes: a face that could struggle, but knew love was
the main thing. Something strangely human about her face; I
think this surprised me. At this point I had perhaps thought
she'd be birdlike.

I cleared my throat as I got close to her, but she didn't stop
talking to them. Ducks, geese and swans, mergansers and
widgeons, swam desultorily around in the pond there before
her, occasionally nibbling on the soggy tossed crumbs. She
spoke to them steadily, softly, in a tone of reassurance, a tone
affectionate and kind.

And here's the strange thing. The unbelievable. As I came
close to the bird chick, so close I could touch her, I discovered
I could understand what it was she said to those birds. The
barrier between myself and that strange tongue fell away, and
I heard the low sweet goodbyes of a bunch of good friends. It
was always like this, the bird chick said, at the end of a show.
Everyone had to disperse. It was one of the tragedies and
beauties of theater. The astonishment created was by nature
impermanent. It couldn't last forever, and it couldn't be
captured. It was a gift given to those who were there. And

after the show was over, that once team – all right, that once family – did what such groups do, that is find their own separate way.

She cried as she said it. The bird chick. So loving of those birds, still so pure after everything. Not wanting to hurt them or chastise them with the course of events.

Stupidly, I still hoped for my autograph. I was getting ready to ask her. But the bird chick stood up then, not even noticing my presence. She dropped her plastic bag and held her arms out wide as if in embrace. Then, with one great dramatic movement, she flung her arms outwards, out towards the waterfowl, hoping to scatter them.

It was her last piece of directing. Like the faithful troupe they had become, they followed her instruction. Out where the great arc of her arms was, those birds flew up in a snow-mist gray cloud, a loud flutter of wings and the honks of their kind. In a slow immense trance they rose over the pond, still to my mind speaking Shakespeare and those lines of the ages.

I watched the miracle of their departing flight and felt a cold grip of sadness alongside my heart. It came to me that we might have to go on without them in our park. They seemed to be flying so far, so determined to leave.

I turned to the bird chick for comfort, no thoughts now of an autograph. I just wanted someone to talk to about the nature of the loss. Right then she seemed to me like anybody else in the park you might strike up some talk with.

But the bird chick was gone. She must have flown too. I don't know why it surprised me — from the start she'd been one to defy the conventions. It made sense that she'd follow her bold gambit into the sky.

Broad from Abroad

Where I live, we have forests. They're like people: tall and short, friendly and crotchety. Here you live among monsters of concrete, their fangs poised overhead, and no one seems to mind or notice. They walk on, like there are better things to worry about.

I like that. I'm always interested in other places' customs.

When I'm abroad, I like to try to fit in. Not take the map out. Get a sense of my bearings and then keep the feet moving, the body in motion, because that's the way you're most likely to avoid what frightens you.

When I first got here I noticed just how much motion there is. Sirens sing and spin and people wave at each other constantly — sometimes in greeting, sometimes with more obscure intentions — when, that is, they aren't knocking against each other like billiard balls and tossing out a quick 'Sorry—' like a handkerchief seen briefly and then carried off by the wind. You can see their thoughts never stopping. There are so many words in people's heads here that they spill out and into the atmosphere, causing a dizzying array of signs to go up everywhere with melancholy phrases like 'last chance sale,' 'You mustn't miss this,' and 'Horne Brothers for men.' I wonder sometimes as I walk which faces on the street chose these particular words, and then I wonder if my thoughts were next to be recorded what they'd read. 'Home – a peaceful place,' maybe, or 'My, but it's loud here.' And, in a good moment: 'Abroad: you should try it.' I can picture the billboards with the slogans.

Elsewhere, great red boats sail down the gray rivers, with people swimming on and off at random, paddling their way over to get on board like a labrador desperately trying to reach the stick that's been thrown out for him in the pond. Paddling, paddling, head in the air, cough-breathing awkwardly, sparkling eyes fixed eagerly on the goal.

When you board the boat, the people seem to get quieter. Out of doors they're chatty, but within they recede into themselves, letting the shuddering, lurching movement of the boat lullaby them into a long-ago childhood. You see them staring out of the window with tears in their usually cynical eyes, fondly remembering that picnic once in the bus shelter or that game they used to play in the hot summer gravel – or whatever it is that people hearken back to here, whatever it is that makes up their past. How can I know that? I'm not like them. Mine's different.

I didn't grow up knowing about boats and galleries, firework displays and the need to stand in a long line of people to receive money, tickets, stamps or forgiveness. Where I grew up we had no lines to stand in and forgiveness was free and plentiful, like weeds – partly because there was so little to be forgiven. As for money or stamps: what would you spend it on? What would you send?

Nothing's more odious, I know, than the non-native pining for home. 'In our country . . .' you say, then close your mouth, knowing they're not interested, knowing that the only people genuinely interested in how life's lived abroad have already gone there, and the ones left behind never cared in the first place. So you keep quiet about life in your country, pretend it's no different, disguise the accent, keep the feet moving, afraid – always afraid! – you might get stuck with what frightens you.

Meanwhile the days hurtle by and your thoughts keep taking you back to the forests. Mine do, at least. I can't help it. I think of Henry, the forest of fig-trees and doves, where occasionally vacations the King of Siam; and I think of Joseph, all pines and firs and the bristle-footed platform of a needle-ground to walk over; I think of Sam, his old oaks and bay trees, buzzards overhead, the red berries of temptation

73

perched sometimes under the claws of the birds. I think, it goes without saying, of Bob – Bob the good and the green, Bob of paper birches and scarlet maples, Bob leading a slow path to the stream there which is blue-silver and kind and tastes of the clean hearts of fish, which have never been known to cause anyone deliberate pain.

But these are memories I must keep to myself.

Here you can't talk about that kind of thing because here the monsters leaning out over everyone have beady electric eyes and elevators running up and down them like blood vessels. Tall buildings. Tall, tall buildings. If you cross them, I've heard, they'll fall all over you, which is why you must at all costs try to ignore them. Don't provoke them by speaking of forests. Don't talk of home. Change the subject. Get along, can't you, be a part of it. So I do it – I keep my mouth shut and pay attention to the local culture. Not wanting to inspire the wrath of the buildings.

What I've seen is this. Every day people groan their way into their jobs here, which exist so that there will be fewer of them out on the street at any one time and so less likelihood of riots or mayhem. They exercise in little, padded, window-less gymnasiums, where they pretend briefly to a life in the country – running, skiing, swimming, cycling their way into infinite space because the idea of really getting anywhere while exercising is anathema. Preposterous – it would be like, the analogy goes, actually walking out of your house and killing a person or violating a person's internal life, instead of doing the sensible thing which is to sit in a dark room with other people watching someone on screen do it instead. Hundreds of thousands of people, I'm told, this way avoid spending their lives in prison because of a crime they might have committed, and are allowed to spend their lives jogging between a dim theater and the brightly lit sanitation of their homes, getting their violence in the one not the other. In this way they remain *free*. Free, in turn, to punch punching bags at the gymnasium.

In their yellow kitchens they unpack plastic and cardboard and foil and paper. They build colorful monuments in a chilly boxed compartment to places that make their mouths water with exotic juices: Chile and Italy, Israel and South Africa, India, France, the Philippines, America. *America*: land of ketchup and corn chips. Home on the range, and amber waves of grain – cornflakes, grapenuts, bran-bits and wheatchex, billowing along the rich aisles and planting a small seed of desire in the hearts of so many children: one day to see that grain, touch that range, drive that car. To go abroad to those countries. To see these foods that speak a hundred different (regulation-bound) languages, all night long, inside the refrigerator.

For the most part, the children here are quite well-behaved and hidden. It is a long apprenticeship into comfort with the life here, and they train the youth busily in small factories designed to produce people who will one day be able to take over the machinery. In this way the entire system provides for itself and is cyclical, wheel-like – in much the same way as several elements of life where I'm from, where perpetuation is the key, where what's small gets bigger in order to come up again with what's small. It's natural, I guess. Self-preservation. The order of things.

What I truly like about life here is the fact that no one ever stops talking. Conversations sprout up out of a floor that looks like cement but apparently isn't, and from these conversations in turn blossom strange wisdoms which give way to the fruits of madness or, in the local vernacular, *art* – great events, you know the ones, where people turn cartwheels on a stage or open their lungs to sing deeply of the ocean and their love lost across it, or draw feathery objects across stringed wood to produce sounds that alter the arrangements of all the atoms in a room. What I mean is, people here dance, shout, play and sing, and all of this is, in my observation anyway, only because first of all there was *talk*.

If I might indulge myself for a moment . . . just for the purpose of putting things in perspective. Because you see in the forests at home, beautiful as they are, there is very little sound, certainly no conversation. If anyone ever asks you this question, as I understand they are likely to, the answer for sure is this: trees falling in the forest never make a sound, whether or not someone's around to hear them, for the simple reason that trees themselves don't believe in making sound. Myself, I find this existence quite peaceful. (I can see that it wouldn't appeal to everyone.) As I mentioned, there is little need in this environment for forgiveness because no one ever says anything to give offense. No one ever says anything at all. While this does have the unfortunate effect of creating a culture without a culture, a land without an art, you must at the same time see the advantages. Think what we live without: anger, scorn, contempt, snobbery, bigotry, stupidity. I won't say it's all love and roses because it isn't. But fewer words means there's so much less pain. Not like here, you know. City of the talking wounded. Folks strapping their ears shut in an effort to heal. It's something worth thinking about, anyway, especially for those of you who've never had the chance to spend much time abroad.

Take Henry, for instance. My good friend Henry. Henry is all figs and doves, sweetness and light. Have you ever seen the platinum glow trapped in the bark of a fig tree, or touched the just-rough excitement of its dinosaur skin? When I'm with Henry the doves land on my shoulder, and if they don't quite coo then they do at least let you press your soft cheek to their downy backs so you feel the warmth of their friendship. This, as I say, is my life with Henry, a life in which we never fight, we merely sit in each other's company and perhaps quietly, internally, philosophize.

With Sam and Joseph it's much the same. Different

personalities, but an equal intimacy that has restored and fed me in the course of years. Joseph, the ascetic – of course, with that name! – pushing me up steep hills with his pine trees and spruces, urging me to the spiritual sort of revelation. Joseph's always had a penchant for angels, gods and spirits. It's the Christmas complex, I believe, what with the fir trees and all. You can hardly blame him. If I walk with Joseph I walk with purer thoughts and leaner struggles – the question perhaps of how to be good, rather than the more metaphysical points with Henry of what makes up the universe. Though when I'm with Joseph being good seems easy.

Sam by comparison is much less demanding. Sam makes me laugh. Sam has never quite grown up, that's what I like about him. He's always enjoyed the sweeter, drier smells and the fun pulse of sunlight. He likes to tease you with snakes and bright butterflies. When you roll around under Sam's oak trees you feel a little playful, a little unserious, a little heady with the sensation that life's young and to be grown in. It could be the bay trees that bring that feeling on. Their deep scent and dark, waxy green leaves, their adult height, their quiet sobriety – remind you of your own youngness, your naïveté. You are a child to those trees, but a happy one.

Bob, of course, is my oldest friend. He, if anyone, pushes the definition of our lives there. Bob's a maverick. It's why we get along. You notice how in what I've said so far there's been no mention of conversation? I'm trying to convey to you

– briefly, I know attention spans are short on this – what it's like in our country, our talkless land of forests. What we miss and how we live. In peace. With greenery. Where the rivers do run blue with water rather than the way they run here, with people and mopeds.

Bob's my oldest friend and the closest to my heart. It might be presumptuous to say I occupy a special place for him, too, but I think it's true. We share an outlook on life. We understand each other.

Bob turns gold in autumn when he's happy, which is for a couple months out of the year when his heart is light and he starts making big plans. As his imagination warms up he turns pumpkin-colored with pleasure and throws pepper-shaded leaves to the ground: red, hot yellow, red-green, amber, ochre, rust. It's so beautiful, what Bob does, even as the air around him slowly slides down in temperature, even as the ice creeps slowly up, as the clouds quiver and chill and try to find new directions. So excited Bob becomes, so triumphant. Saying nothing, you realize. Just shaking out the forest's limbs sometimes in the fall's salt breezes and on those breezes sending messages about hue and why and the importance of vividness. Bob's nothing if not vivid. People think he's sad when he goes through this. There are those who still don't understand Bob, and it's not just you foreigners I mean, sometimes even the natives fail to see what he's up to. They don't understand what a gift it is, what a celebration. What a performance it is really, what an acting out of some of the truer, better moments of the spirit. Of Bob's spirit.

It *is* art. I have to say this, because I love Bob and Bob is my friend. Someone has to stand up for him, point out how great his work is. It is art, this autumnal procession, this concert, this dance to the season. Deep down I think we all know it is.

But it frightens me, always, every year. I say this too in friendship. Because always, afterwards, after the performance, there's a still bareness and an emptiness of leaves. There's an overall brownness. (A gray, even, in a bad year.) All the bounty has become the forest floor, where it will of course rot and go to the bugs and salamanders, and there's little left in the air to look at except the bitter, thin glory of plain branches.

And this is what frightens me. This is what I try to avoid, if you must know. This is why I come abroad, to your country, to your place, strange as it is with its boats and its busloads and its buy, buy, buy.

Because where I come from, after Bob's art there is silence. We have no conversation. We have no talk. We don't even have any applause — not the sound of one hand clapping, or of two. All we have is silence. Silence is the good, we believe, it's life as it should be.

But when you've seen the beauty there that I've seen, you need to talk about it. You can't help it. A heart must bear witness. A voice has to shout at the splendor and the pain of living through that kind of artwork. This is why I come to these streets here to walk around – much as I miss everybody at home while I'm gone, much as I look forward to Bob's leafy embrace when I return. I know here that my own chatter of despairing praise will go unnoticed in the great clamor of people hoping to be heard. I duck under the tall buildings, and I speak my mind.

The Girl in the Red Chair

It sometimes seemed that the chair was louder than her, but in fact she was louder than the chair.

A screamer she was. Loud as red. My, but that girl had a fine pair of lungs.

Fortunately she used them to good effect. She didn't shout about just anything. I mean, not the kinds of things you or I tend to shout about: high prices, the rise in divorce rates, badly behaved movie stars and slow public transportation. The number of times you find gum on your shoe just from walking around the streets like any normal person does.

No, no, her subjects were far more lofty and significant. Regularly her themes were kindness, fairness, art. The import-ance of affection. The value of sunlight. How to stay fit while still keeping friendly and interesting. Things that could lift you up – if you were in the mood to be lifted up, if you weren't too busy (don't you have moments like this?) worrying about that shoe.

Her father had been an encyclopedia salesman. That's where she got it from, her oratorical skill. She spent her entire childhood with him, sitting in the cab of his pick-up truck as they drove from one end of the country to the other selling encyclopedias. He was a smooth talker: he dazzled the housewives. They never knew before they met him just how much there was to know. They never knew you could cram everything important into two heavy lumps of reconstituted forest. They hadn't guessed that living with an encyclopedia or without one could make the difference between raising an axe-murderer and raising somebody elegant and competent who in future years might take expeditions along the Nile, spouting off about the ancient process of mummification. The knowledge was cheap at the price – they had to agree.

The girl was brought along by the father to reassure the ladies. She never said anything. She just stood flat-footed on their porches admiring the soft velvet red of their begonias while her father hypnotized and chided. If the women were worried about the strange man coming to their door, the girl was around to reassure them. If the women were excited about a strange man coming to their door, she was there to dampen their enthusiasm. Though if it came to it she was able to make herself scarce, playing with the tiger cat in the garden, until her father came back out refreshed and ready to leave again. She'd bring cat hair and the memory of other species with her back into the cab, which would smell flowery for a short while after, of women's perfume. She and her father mostly communicated on those journeys through song. They had a repertoire of thirty or forty jaunty, sometimes melancholy tunes they knew that got them through all their travels, making conversation all but unnecessary.

By the time they'd reached the coast at the other end of the country she was grown up, the truck was fixing to retire, and her father was grizzled though nonetheless charming still when you got him going on the subject of encyclopedias. She tipped her hat to him – a stetson she'd picked up en route – and thanked him for the journey, before going along on her own separate way.

It was not so clear to her at first what her role in the world was supposed to be now. With her stetson and her toothbrush she walked up and down the big city streets, hopping on a bus every now and then and keeping her eyes peeled for opportunities. She finally found one in an art gallery, of all places. They said they liked the look of her there. They spoke with strange accents that sounded foreign to her, though she realized that she must in fact be the foreigner. They told her they liked her look of integrity; that she seemed like the kind of person who could not be bought. She agreed with this, though she didn't actually know what she'd have said if someone tried to buy her.

They used her there to model the artwork. She was happy to do it on the condition that they let her keep her hat on at all times. They had to agree, though it was against their policy. Secretly they were thrilled because this was further proof of her integrity.

It was a simple, gratifying job that involved wearing the artwork and allowing people to come in and look at it, and you, and discuss them both, and analyze the form of it, and then the content, and then the morality, and then the politics, and then the implications and so on right on down to whether they actually liked the piece or not. Sometimes the girl found it hard not to laugh at what was said but she absolutely was not allowed to laugh and would lose her job if ever she did. Sometimes she wanted just to sigh – she wasn't allowed to do that either – because there was a streak of cruelty that ran through the people that came in there and even on a day when what she wore was a work fabulously, brilliantly red that made her own soul soar and flutter and beat its wings in the clouds – even on that day a couple came in, looked at it, looked at her, shrugged their shoulders and said loudly, 'Derivative.'

It was a long crash landing for her ideals that afternoon and she had to let the sigh out in little measured breath-like gasps so that no one would hear her.

One day a young man came in alone to see her. He wore a black leather jacket and carried a notebook. He wasn't with anyone so he didn't say anything. This was frustrating to her because the look he had on his face was intelligent and she felt sure that he was seeing something unusual in that day's artwork, and she was very curious to know what it was. Everyone else but her, everyone who came in to see the art, was of course allowed to sigh or gasp or snort or make whatever noise they chose. He came out with something like a whimper at one point – when a spasm of sadness crossed his face – and then a sound like a snicker, when he thought of something funny and joy lit a green light in his eye. He took out his notebook and started writing, absorbed in what he did, chuckling every now and then at his own reflections.

The girl was ready to wail with frustration. Generally her job didn't make her feel powerless – she felt she was serving an important function there at the gallery, and anyway she always had her hat on to comfort her – but just then she came to see that she was a scarecrow and nothing else and that people think of scarecrows as stuffed canvas bags or dummies, certainly not as potential friends, and that that must be how this man in the leather jacket thought of her too.

He looked up as this thought of hers completed itself – his hand still grasping his pen, the pen waiting over the page for its next instruction, his brain rustling around for the phrase he was looking for, his eyes wandering here and there as if somehow they might be able to bring aid to his brain.

His eyes caught hers, and brightened. 'Caution, speed bumps!' he said out loud with an air of triumph.

She laughed, and was fired.

Naturally they went home together, as he was responsible for her losing her position. He was sorry about that, but she asked him not to apologize as she'd really gotten everything from that job she was going to get and it was time for her to move on.

They went ahead and fell in love. It was beautiful. Daffodils and sparkplugs, wine bottles and puddle-jumping, giggling deep into a maroon night at the silly splendors of the world. Rolling in goose feathers, coffee in bed. Stories from childhood shaken out from dusty cabinets of memory. The soft touch of fingers. The hot song of red lips.

After that they set up shop together. It was an ambition of both of theirs. She still lived always in her stetson. He was wise enough to see that the hat for her was like his notebook was for him — something sacrosanct, a mysterious, private vessel that contained all the wit and weirdness of a person's interior world. He wouldn't have dreamed of asking her to share or change it.

They lived in a part of town where many different cultures collided, not always happily, and though this was an advantage for restaurants, it posed a slight problem for them businesswise as mostly what they sold in their shop were stories and peanuts. From the beginning the peanuts sold better than the stories.

As I say, this might have been due to the neighborhood. They were his stories exclusively, written in his native language, and though they always made the girl laugh and she thought everyone would love them, the fact was the people who came into the store there looked through the stories, maybe even chuckled a little over them, but then saw the peanuts and left only with those.

The two were optimistic at first that they could change those patterns. He and the girl tried a few different marketing-type strategies. They displayed the peanuts behind an unappealing formica counter where people would have to ask for them specially, while the stories were left lying around on polished wood tables, just asking to be read. They – or rather, she – designed attractive covers for the stories to make them enticing. They put on promotional sales. Buy two stories get the third one free, that kind of thing. These measures always worked briefly and they'd get their hopes up, and then people would go back to their old ways, buying mostly peanuts.

The atmosphere became very dispiriting in there. He was miserable, obviously. When she first met him in the art gallery he had had a sound about him, a humming in his eyes so you knew he was watching things, and his leather jacket crackled with pleasure at the physical world. Now his eyes and his jacket wore the same dull darkness, his stubble grew for days at a time, he barked when he asked for things and he seemed at times to forget her name.

She was inclined to hit the road with him. That was the life she knew best and she felt that the road was good for lifting people's spirits and bringing them out of themselves. After all, it had cured her own father of whatever lifelong illness he'd had. (Before he'd been an encyclopedia salesman he'd lived his life in a suit and an office, blind as a potato.) The wide, blank spaces of the road and the cornfields, the changing dimensions of the blue and dark sky, the consistencies and inconsistencies of the people you met – all of these things brought a person away from his or her hoarded despair and back into the absurdity and sometime pleasure of a world which included other people. He needed to be reminded of this absurdity, she felt, since the people in the store just struck him as narrow-minded fools, and he'd all but stopped noticing the girl herself.

Before she could broach the subject he had decided without her. She woke in the room they lived in behind the store one morning and found a stack of his manuscripts beside her with a little postcard on top. The postcard was a picture of an automobile, red. The card was very beautifully written. It said that he was in one of these now (see picture) not because he didn't love her or want to live with her or think her a jewelled being, but because he needed the redness and mobility and throb of a car to save him from the acts of disappointment he'd begun to dream of committing. He said he was going to drive until he no longer wanted to commit them, until he couldn't even remember what it was like to be a person cold and forgetful or sour with bile. The card made her cry. In her new life in this store, which hadn't been easy but had been a good life nonetheless, one with a great share of sweetness and affection, in this new life she was allowed to react to things and so she shut up shop for the day, posted a sign that said 'Bereavement' in the window and tried to figure out what to do with herself next.

This was right around the time I met her, so you see I didn't meet the girl at her best. She was very thin when I met her, and lines of concern pinched the edges of her face. It was an accident that I did meet her. We bumped into each other on a street corner, apologized, then realized that we each looked vaguely familiar to the other. It turned out I'd once been in the store buying a story and some peanuts. (For what it's worth, I thought his writing was good. He turned a phrase nicely, but I guess that's not always enough in these hard times.) Not only that, she'd once been in my furniture store eyeing some sofas. I think this was one of the few clandestine activities she indulged in when she lived with the boy.

There was no question of her continuing to run the store without him. She was holding a closing down sale and was going to get rid of all the merchandise. Half-price stories, peanuts at cost. It made her too sad, she said. Reminded her too much of him. She said all this in almost a whisper. At that point I thought she was one of the softest spoken girls I'd ever met in my life. I remember saying as much to my husband. I'd never have believed someone then telling me what she would later become.

All she really wanted, the girl told me, was a chair. A big red chair – the biggest and reddest one we had. She had decided against a sofa, she said. She wanted something that would keep her relatively upright. She was conscientious that way. So I sold her a chair on excellent terms. My husband always had to remind me, 'This is a business not a charity' – though in these days people need charity more than they need business, in my opinion – so I couldn't outright give the thing to her, which I was tempted to do because she looked so frail and depressed. What I could do was give her free delivery. I'm sure she appreciated it.

She disappeared then for almost a whole year, and I just about forgot she existed. As far as I know, she had a long sleep. She had a lot to recover from, you see, what with the art gallery and then the love affair and then the retail worries and then his going. If you'd ever seen her in that red chair then – her slight frame shrunk into the deep, frothy, vocal red of it – you could picture how she might get swallowed up by it and just doze off for a year or so, letting the chair make all the noise for her and support her in her time of silence.

I heard about her again finally when she woke up and started talking to herself. A friend of mine asked me had I heard about that red chair girl carrying on uptown and I thought, it can't be the same person, but as it turned out it was. I guess that sleep must have been what she needed because she came out of it shouting. Shouting, and a little bit bigger, and, it seemed, with a much improved appetite.

Not everyone liked what she said, because she wasn't necessarily the kind of person who made you feel great and secure and happy about everything. But everyone wanted to hear her. They'd caught the rumor, which was true, that once you heard her the first time somehow you had to go back and hear her again because you needed to settle a few lasting doubts you had about the sound of her voice, or the depth of her message. Before you knew it you kept going back. And once you became a regular (as I did, of course – feeling connected to her career because of the early assistance I gave her) you'd see the same faces reappearing. You'd nod to each other knowingly, smiling that club-like smile. These were people from all different walks of life. People there got to know each other a little, a plumber and a lawyer for instance, people who might not otherwise have found common ground for conversation.

I should say that the girl in the red chair didn't ask for an audience. I don't think she expected one. It always seemed to me that she was surprised when she opened her eyes and realized there were people around her listening. If there was

95

anyone she focussed on it was only the tiger cat she had acquired some time in that year, who now slept and purred on her lap while she delivered her words. And, of course, for the most part her remarks were addressed not to any of us, but to the man who had left her and was somewhere out in his car. It seemed as if there were many things she wished she'd said to him and never had, probably because at first they were too busy enjoying their love and their bed together to talk of the other kinds of grand questions, and then later because he was too gloomy and downtrodden to be able to sustain that level of engagement. Now, even in her small set of experiences of the world (which she detailed for us so we'd understand the connection), she'd come to see that she had opinions about the importance of community and the great need for fellow feeling; about the nastiness and brutality all around her, and how that must not be allowed or glossed over; about the significance of friendship and of listening to the words and works of the others. Opinions, all of them, that she had gleaned from her experiences in art and in commerce, opinions that came in part from her life and the unkindnesses she'd seen, opinions that she wanted to express now, that was all, that she wanted (she was shouting) to *give voice to now*.

The chair, around her, lost some of its redness on her especially loud days. You'd have thought, so insistent was she, that she wanted to sell you something. (I could have used her in my store, that's for sure, with that kind of pitch!)

It was a plea to be in the world, I think. Having listened to her for quite a while, having gotten the facts, such as there were, of her story, this is what seemed to me to be her overarching concern: she wanted you to listen to other people's tales. Not even buy them, necessarily, but listen at least. And it was a plea not to fall down with discouragement if folks couldn't at first hear you. The thought was to keep talking and listening, till a conversation got going. The girl encouraged people to shout back at her about this. She wanted engagement. And, you know, quite a few of them did shout back. It wasn't enough, she would say, to inhabit just a truck cab or an art gallery or a story store. Life – and she should know this, she spent a year sleeping on the question – was about adventuring into the world, mixing it up, sniffing out the unhappy people out there and shouting them into talk, because that was how as a group we might just about stay together.

It wasn't for our benefit that she shouted all this, though we did benefit from it. I personally know several people who changed their jobs after they heard her; or who took the unfamiliar step of listening to their children; or who went out to dinner with their friends and boldly asked them some questions. I believe this was because of her exhortations. Because she asked you to look up from your shoes.

In her big old stetson – she still had it, weatherbeaten though it was now – she cut an odd figure in that plum tomato chair, stroking the tigery back of her cat. Sometimes quiet and small, deceptively timid, like the last thing she wanted was to disturb anyone's peace. Sometimes you couldn't believe this little person actually had so much rage in her, and you couldn't quite remember where it all came from. Then sometimes her great lungs so exercised themselves that the shop windows – where she used to put little enticing displays of peanuts, back in the good old days when they were still together running the store – shook and quivered with the immensity of her voice.

I hope he hears it one day, and comes back to be with her. Who knows what route he may be on, in which of the many states there are out there? Who knows if he's let go of his old disappointment? I just hope he does hear her and decide to come back. It's not that I don't like to listen to all her wise yelling, it's just that I'm worried one day she might shout herself hoarse.

Mistress of Many Moons

Well, not *so* many. People do like to exaggerate. It makes a better story that way – sells more magazines.

. . .

Oh, you know, the story of someone like me, who's had one moon after the other, or maybe some different moons at the same time even, and of course each time I must get all their secrets, and so I must be one of the best-informed etcetera of all moons *everywhere*, what with all that privileged access . . . (laughs)

. . .

Well, yes, it may be true to *some* extent. Yes. I suppose I shouldn't be so flip about it. Yes, I mean if you wanted to ask me about a particular moon, that moon's favorite color, or the movie that most influenced them, or the orbit they would keep if they could have their druthers – oh, I could give you all that. But I know you're much too discreet to ask me such things.

. . .

Of course, politics, too. Yes, of course. Now that really would be out of bounds, wouldn't it? But yes, for instance there was one moon – I'm sure you know the one I mean – whose opinion on the Slmovian situation at the time *everyone* was after. Should we pull out, or should we delve further in? Should we drop bombs, or should we send over a vanfull of diplomats? What's the plan? What's the strategy? ——But that moon was much too smart to say a word or predict the future (I think that's what the press were expecting, truthfully). So it was me who was left blinking at flashbulbs, caught in my evening wear, looking foolish as I blurted out, 'I don't know! I don't have the moon's opinion about it! I mean, if you ask me, live and let live, but I guess that's not the answer you're looking for!' They never let me forget that one. Oh, no! '*Mistress pouts, "Life is for living!" ——Refuses to give up social life to aid Slmovian refugees.*' I swear to you that was one story that got printed. They do like to distort – I should say *you* like to distort, since you're one of them too, don't think I haven't noticed.

. . .

Oh, yes. 'Life is for living.' I ask you. Does that sound like a motto for our times? Even for someone as notorious as myself? Why not just quote me as saying, 'Drink Polka Cola'? It would have been about as accurate.

. . .

Endorsements? Are you kidding?

. . .

Who do you think would want me to endorse them? Cleaning products? Tennis shoes? The beleaguered space agency?

. . .

(laughs) Well. It's a wonderful idea. Maybe you should suggest it to them. But no, I've never been approached by anybody, including the space agency, to do PR for them. Though they do need it now, don't they, poor dears? They're always blowing themselves up by accident or putting on the nosecone backwards. One of these days there's going to be a blast-off and the rocket's going to go straight down into the earth instead. A whole new era of subterranean exploration will begin. All because the space agency people had their instructions upside down.

No, but there's a serious question behind what you ask and it's to do with how the space agency deals with moons, actually, and by extension with someone like me, and I have to tell you that their policy has consistently been to pretend, in this absurd way, that none of us *exist*. It's part of their whole ostrich mentality. As if these moons weren't genuine moons, as though even if you found their existence embarrassing to admit you couldn't just pull me aside, on the sly, and ask me informally, 'So what is it that moons are really like, eh? I mean, we have all this fancy measuring equipment and telescopes and cloudometers and whatever, but what's the inside scoop on life as a moon?' —In that case, you see, I would have been perfectly willing to tell them, to really spill the beans, pardon the expression, on moonlife, moonlove, moontalk, etcetera. If it was for *science* I'd be happy to be quite forthright, and I don't think of that as being indiscreet at all. Just public interest, for science.

But they never approached me, so what can I say? It's their loss. They're wedded to their machines. They're all paid so much to manipulate their technology they forget there's such a thing as a human angle on these stories.

. . .

No, thank you, that's not the reason. I've already told you I've gotten as much publicity myself as I could ever want. No, I honestly think, and I know someone like me is not supposed to have a brain and it complicates the story if it turns out I do have one, but I honestly think that the space agency is missing out on a lot of important information about the universe, and that if they don't pull themselves together one of these days to explore these other avenues they're just going to keep on building imploding aircraft, one after the other, and sending people off into black holes by mistake.

Incidentally, just to underline the point that it's not about my self-glorification, I'm not the only one around to talk to.

Not to lessen my interview fees, heaven forbid, but there are others around who've been intimate with moons.

. . .

I'm not going to tell you that! You'll have to find out for yourself who they are. That's your job. Investigation. Isn't that part of your job? Or is your job really just to flatter people into confessions and then savage them later through innuendo and editing?

. . .

Yes, let's change the subject. To what?

. . .

Marriage? Oh dear. Really?

. . .

(sigh) No. I never did. That is the truth. I never wanted to because, let's face it, what happens to wives of moons? You get attached to their fancy orbit and become invisible. People actually start to look through you, right back into the dark space in the background. (They'll notice the constellations, but they won't notice you.) I'll tell you the two times you're visible if you marry a moon: one, on the day of the wedding, when the flashbulbs circle round you like haloes and the papers declare you glorious and radiant; and the other, the day the divorce is announced, when the flashbulbs hover over you like vultures and the going adjectives are 'distraught' and 'haggard.' Thanks, but I'd prefer to earn 'haggard' the hard way, on my own, with respect to my own achievements or lack of them.

People seem to think that with some moons – you know, the liberated ones, the 'nice ones' – that there is some suggestion that you could have your own orbit, and it could be separate from theirs, and that would be okay, no one would have a problem with that. This is patently ridiculous. Have you ever known that to actually work? Have you ever known a moon, in fact, who didn't like to hog the limelight? I may sound bitter here, but I don't mean to. I've lived the life I have because I *love* moons, they can and should have *lots* of limelight; I mean they're beautiful, wonderful, dazzling – of course! I have a weakness for moons!

But there comes a time with a moon when you can tell that it's not going to work out. You can just sense it. And at that point it's best to slip out and off into your own pattern of movement. Which is much easier to do if you're a mistress. And all but impossible to do if you're a wife.

. . .

Ah, well, *love* . . .

Are you sure this is the point in the interview where you want to ask about that? Are you ready to see me get all weak-kneed and melty?

. . .

All right. Love.

Let's see, what was that moon's name again? (laughs) No, no. Just kidding.

I do like to tell this story in fact. It's terribly romantic.

First, in answer to the first part of your question, yes, of course love is a player in all these stories, in all the encounters I've had with moons – not *so* many, remember, not so very many! – but mostly it hasn't been that movie kind of love; it's been more of a brief, planetary kind of love. It's hard to explain if you've never experienced it. It is as though there is this immense, irresistible pull between you – some of those old clichés, *magnetism*, for example, describe it perfectly – and while there is this pull you are devoted to that moon, you would do anything for that moon, you'd be happy to live in that moon's shadow for the rest of eternity. It's that feeling, of course, that leads to people getting married. Fortunately, I always know, in a tiny pocket of my heart, that this feeling will pass, and so while it lasts we love and we adventure and we sing our music of the stars – and it is all very pure and happy and there are no strings attached.

But I did fall in love once. That way. The way you're thinking, what you have in mind when you ask me that question. How did I recognize the difference? It was the walk we took along the river one night. This is a beautiful story. I've told it before – but, if you're lucky, not for quite a few years so your readers won't remember it. Anyway, we were walking along the famous river in that famous city and it was several years ago – don't ask me how many! – and so the traffic was silenced. In those days they never used to let traffic interfere with important moments like these: the romance of riverwalks, the still of the dark. Now of course the traffic's all-important, to hell with everyone else. And they wonder why romance is dying.

Anyway, it was indigo and hushed and the only beat you heard was my heels on the pavement. Our hearts were loud in our own ears – mine was, anyway – so loud we couldn't hear the other's. The trees by the river played their special night music: a low, breezy rhythm, the soft tune of the leaves. My lips kept moving as if to say something, but my throat was too nervous and wouldn't open up. Then the moon did the thing that moons do best, that can seem very trite unless it's being done just for you, in which case it is incredibly moving! The moon shone on the water – shone mercury and opal – lit the surface of that river with elements I'd heard of before but never seen for myself. The moon spoke to me in minerals, in micas and phosphorites, chromium and cinnabar. It was a new poetry to me, this trick of the lighting. I shouldn't say 'trick.' This moon was sincere. But for someone like me – who'd been wined and dined plenty, given flowers and chocolates, but never addressed in this way, in this strange, subtle language – the effect was overwhelming. I felt my head spinning, as if off its axis; my eyes became galaxies that took in the world. The colors in the water went way beyond what I could possibly know – to manganese and willemite, zircon, olivine and feldspar. The moon was giving back to me, I realized, the nature of our earth. And this sonnet had my name on it, the

moon meant it for *me*. I can tell you, I fell in love that night –
feeling loved, I mean really loved, for the first time in my life.
That's how it works, I've come to believe. (I've had a lot of
time to think about it since.) Someone speaks something that
touches you, that recognizes what's deeply in you and makes
it seem glorious. The passion that wakes up then is like
nothing else.

. . .

What? Oh. (pause) Yes. I'm never allowed to end the story
there, am I? The interview can never just end there.

Well. It was love, purely. It was love and then fate, or the
cosmos or whatever you want to call it, intervened. The moon
had to leave. The moon was drawn in another direction – one
I just couldn't follow.

. . .

No. (snaps) *Couldn't*. Couldn't, literally, follow. This moon
had an orbit that would take it someplace I couldn't even
breathe. I know there is a thought that if you're truly in love
you would lay down your life . . . But what would have been
the point of that, an oxygenless death? No, that was it. We
simply had to separate. The moon, grieving, told me to stay,
insisted we'd never forget each other. It's true. I've never
forgotten. I'll go to my grave thinking of silver and cinnabar,
with that one long night etched in my bloodstream.

. . .

Such melodramas. You want to write that? Go ahead. You

can write 'Her heart was broken after that.' What do I care what you write? In fact, of course, it still works, which is why I'm living and breathing and here to tell you the story. And if you look up the chronology I'm afraid you'll discover I've had other moons since.

Look, you asked me about love so that's what I told you. I apologize if it doesn't fit the shape that you wanted.

. . .

No. It sounds strange, but it didn't. I've always loved moons, and understood the lives that they lead. One experience or another doesn't change my opinion. Because in fact it's not an opinion at all, it's rather the shape of my heart. I guess some people will think this sounds terribly arrogant or something, but I've just never had a feeling for the ordinary earth-bound types. I don't mean that how it sounds. I don't mean 'Oh everyone on earth is so boring and plain, give me a planet, give me someone who shines in the dark.' Of course I'm aware that that's how a lot of people think of me. There's a phrase for people like me, isn't there? For people who – but it's got that very crude word in it that I know you can't print so I won't bother saying it. You know the phrase I'm talking about?

Anyway, it really isn't that way with me at all. I just feel more comfortable in the company of moons. Always have. Always loved moons, even as a child. Always hankered after them. My mother wasn't pleased about it – let's not go into my mother in this interview, all right? You can read through your clips for it, it's in there in triplicate, I bet. She thought I'd be unhappy for the rest of my life. By her standards, I probably have been. But by my standards – and those are the ones that count, in this instance! – I've been happy. I've lived a full life. I've taken in the glow of these moons – not *so* many, not so many! – and I've had the fast heartrate of life in deep space; I've known the laughter of asteroids and understood the call of coyotes at midnight. It's been an incredibly rich life. A passionate one. And yes, I know secrets, many secrets of moons. Your boss – your editor – will be disappointed that you didn't get more of them out of me, but just tell your editor that I was a crotchety, senile old so-and-so and wouldn't cough up. It's not so far from the truth, after all.

. . .

(sings) '. . . I've had a few, but then again, too few . . .' (laughs)

No, that's not true. There are a few regrets I want to mention. That I never got my own TV show; that they never named a sandwich after me, or a cocktail; that I probably won't make it into *Who's Who*.

No, I'm just fooling with you. People really do expect answers like that though. They expect that, or the old saw about having children, and I have to say I find both of those lines of thought clogged and uninteresting. Find someone else to ask about having children. Ask some of those moons . . .

No. The single regret I have is a strange, unreal regret. The thing I regret is that I wasn't a moon myself. That I never, through all these years, somehow became a moon – by osmosis, you know, by being around so many of them. I think in my heart I always hoped, dreamed it would happen. I dreamed I would wake up one day, glowing like a great coin, all round and big and casting my influence on the tides. This I think was my dream. It explains why I have always loved moons so. It even explains – this may be too complicated for you, but see if you can get it – why I never wanted to marry one. To marry a moon, somehow, would be to admit that you weren't one yourself. That you had to be satisfied with attaching yourself to the side of one. Do you understand what I mean? Being a mistress you can sustain the other illusion. That you are the same, at base. That you have moon-ness in you. This is why I've been close to so many, but always stayed free.

It's the best life I could have had, with the strange things I wanted. I wouldn't change five minutes of it. Wouldn't have loved less, couldn't have loved more. I'm just lucky to have had the knack I did for carrying on my life almost solely in moonlight.

. . .

Yes, let's. I think that's all there is to say.

. . .

Thank you, that's gracious of you, even if it may not be true. So did I. Now, though, I'm tired out.

Would you like something to drink? Let's turn that thing off and sit out on the balcony. You can hear the ocean from out there. It's soothing and pretty. As you must know, it sounds like somebody close to you, breathing.

She Who Caught Buses

She Who Caught Horses

There was a bunch of Chranks at the bus stop today. All standing together the way they do. Talking amongst themselves. They speak so fast sometimes it sounds like a dialect.

My policy is to ignore them. I figure if I ignore them, they'll leave me alone. They won't even notice me, probably. That's the way I prefer it.

The bus came at last – not a minute too soon. Shaking and steaming, coughing like someone with emphysema. All the Chranks bunched up behind me, waiting for me to get on. I felt like I was being herded. I wondered if this was what sheep feel like when some creature's worrying them.

Not that the Chranks worry me, I mean. I wouldn't give them that satisfaction.

Once you're on the bus, I find, things calm down. I always

feel safer there. I look out of the window at yellow fields of corn and sunshine alternating with the big city blocks, and I feel confident that everything will be fine that day. No one can get to you on the bus. If anyone tries anything funny, there's always the driver sitting up there all fat in his uniform, observing everyone to keep them in line. Even the belligerent ones. The whole scene makes me feel at home, like I can genuinely relax for at least the course of the journey. To tell you the truth, I feel safer on the bus than anywhere else in my life. Yes, really: safer there than in my own bed at home; than out on these pigeon-gray streets; than in the diner where I go for coffee and sandwiches. Even than in my own job, at the library, where I spend most of my days stamping and staring.

In fact the library where I work seethes with discomfort and dangers. You may laugh – people think I exaggerate – but the fact is everyone spies on each other there, everyone's trying to figure out everyone else's secret. The problem in the library is that you're not allowed to talk there. You know the rules in libraries. No verbal clues: only hidden assessments. This is both the blessing and the curse of life in the library. The good news is that you need never be exposed to the horrific range of opinions held by the majority of your customers; the downside is that you have no way of telling, finally, which ones are Chranks. If there's never even a moment of that unmistakable dialect, never a breath of that odd rhythm of their tongue, you have only your own wit and experience to go by to determine who's who. Sometimes I look at the shape of the brow: a particular kind of slope, like the face of a grapefruit, is a reliable indicator. A pencil moustache on the men is another characteristic; polka-dotted clothes worn by the women is also a good sign. (Both sexes, as you know, display the tendency to burst into loud song, but that's not the kind of thing you'll hear done in a library.) Sadly, until I'm sure – until I'm *really sure* – I have to check out their books and smile as if they were just anybody. This is the galling, stressful aspect of my job – constantly worrying that I might be handing over a great work, perfectly friendlily, to someone who actually comes from the tribe of the Chrank. Does a Chrank deserve Kafka, I ask you? Or *The Sickness Unto Death*? How about Salinger or the love poems of Sappho? Should Chrank children have the privilege of Gallico's *Jennie* or the melting snowball of Keats' *Snowy Day*? It is not for me to make these judgments, of course, and I know that. I am a librarian and I am not God. Still, one can use the small power of a job like mine to quietly influence and favor, and I spend the better part of my moral energy trying to do just that.

People say this is a fixation of mine, that I'm clearly obsessed. On lunchbreaks in the diner I've heard co-workers mutter. 'She's got a bee in her bonnet about Chranks,' one of them said. 'She can't let it go.' I was sipping a malted milk on that particular day and pretending not to listen. But I think the other one saw my ears twitching and lowered her voice. I only caught phrases after that, but they didn't make me happy. '. . . Keeps to herself . . . excessive interest . . . warped mentality . . . I think she's prejudiced.'

It's that last word that bothers me. The rest goes with the territory of keeping your own counsel and having an inquisitive mind. People don't like you to keep your library silences outside the library. The common expectation is that after a morning of silence you'll have plenty to say. Whereas just the opposite tends to be true for me. I find the less I speak, the less I want to. Vocal chords rust in place. The effort begins to seem painful. I forget, even, on a bad day, which movement of the lips effects exactly what phrase. Needless to say, this does not make me popular. You are encouraged, actually just this side of forced, to split sandwiches with others and chat about life. Whereas my tendency has always been to pursue in my breaktimes the activity that I am tortured to watch everyone else do all day: fondle a plump plastic-wrapped volume, crack its often-cracked back and spread open the pages. Swallow what's there, whatever it is. Devour the words. I read all I can, in short, on my lunchbreaks while the other girls sit around coffee cups gabbing. They're bound not to like it. They're bound to tell tales.

Prejudiced, however, is one thing I'm not. And if I ever had the chance – if I could ever make myself do it – I would tell those people, those women I work with, the truth about Chranks and how unfair it is to leap to conclusions about someone like me. 'Prejudiced': people throw the word around like it's a hot potato, hold it in their palms for a second before realizing how burning and hurtful it is, then toss it on to someone else in the hope that they'll be stupid enough to catch. It's not a nice game, I want to tell them. Don't make me play.

If they would listen, this is what I would tell them. It's a story about Chranks. A real story, mine, not something I read.

Because when I was a child I didn't actually live here. Not here amidst the cornfields and the banks, the bundled-up hay and the once-a-year fair. Where I grew up, some ways from here, there was a deep, gray pond and a nest full of owls. The road out of our house was more like a track. The schoolbus, when it showed up, was yellow and bulbous and looked out of place and modern in the midst of that country.

When you grow up in a place like that of course you can't be picky about your friends. This is why it's so ridiculous to say that I'm prejudiced. When I was a youngster I smiled and spoke to everything that lived and breathed. I had to – otherwise I'd have had no company whatsoever, and in that case I would truly have grown up to be strange.

My best friends at that stage were a family of owls and a persimmon tree in our yard, and then – controversially – the person who lived at the bottom of the pond. None of these friendships were what you'd call easy. The owls, for example, kept very different hours from myself and so arranging a time to meet could be quite complicated. All during my schoolday and afternoon they were fast asleep in their nest. Just as they woke up, I was generally brushing my teeth before bedtime. Our finest hours were right around dawn, when I'd be bleary-eyed with what my dreaming had brought to me all through the night and their beaks would be bloodied still with bits of their prey. At that point we could sit around, all of us together, and at least catch each other up on the previous night and the day. I think we all got something out of it: the interest in learning what life was like in the light, or, the other way around, how it felt to fly in the dark.

The persimmon tree and I had even more trouble communicating, and I think this was really a case more of mutual admiration than genuine friendship. Persimmons are near-human, I don't know if you know this: their long shape and rich reddish color make them more like an organ than any other fruit. There is something moving in this (I recognized it even when I was young). As for what the tree liked about me: perhaps it was the gold stars and smiley faces I brought home from my schoolteachers, which I magnanimously shared and stuck on its branches.

But the figure in this story lived at the bottom of the pond, and this was the main figure from my childhood. The figure had a face and a body and, as far as I ever knew, a home there, at the bottom of the pond, though my parents told me I wasn't allowed to visit. This figure and I were able nonetheless to play together quite happily, even to have brisk conversations. With its bright green eyes and intelligent expression the figure was attractive, in its way, and showed a good sense of humor.

'What did you do today?' the figure might ask me.

'Pledge allegiance to the flag. The usual stuff.'

'Which flag is that?'

'*Our* flag, silly!' The figure had a tendency to be uninformed when it came to the basics. 'Redwhitenblue.'

'Why does this flag want your allegiance? What's it planning to do?'

'Nothing. It's not the flag that wants it, it's our teacher.'

'I thought you said it was the flag.'

'We *say* it to the flag.'

'Well, what does the flag say back?'

'Nothing!'

'Nothing at all?'

'Of course not!'

'How arrogant. And how rude. While all of you stand up and pledge your allegiance to it! And what does the teacher say?'

'"Thank you."'

'I should think so, too. Still, I don't like it.'

'What?'

'The whole business,' the figure would say, then change the subject.

And with these conversations we covered much of the ground of my school life, with the figure pointing out inconsistencies here and there in the curriculum, and the futility of certain stories like the one about pilgrims. As the figure pointed out, no one really seemed to wear those hats any more, the ones we laboriously made out of colored paper and cardboard, which must say something about the lack of real puritan influence; and furthermore it was not well explained, the whole meaning of 'religious persecution.' What with the way the Indians fitted in and with the missions and all, the figure was of the opinion that the whole founding fathers story didn't add up.

It was the course of these discussions I think that led me to my desire for more learning and books. The figure was very well-read and not shy about sharing its knowledge with me the way grown-ups generally were. Adults, I remember noticing at the time, are so in love with the power of knowledge that it delights them best to dispense it in bite-sized pellets. They are not eager to feed the ones with big appetites. They prefer to educate with that thin weak stream of gruel.

I'm getting to the part about Chranks, don't worry, they are about to join in on this story. They appeared just as I was deciding that it would really probably be best if I disobeyed my parents on this single occasion and went down to the bottom of the pond to take a look at the library. The figure, I knew, had an amazing library down there – much greater, obviously, than the scrawny little one at our school, which was papered with pumpkins and ponies and other degrading icons of childhood. The figure itself did not take a stand on my excursion to the library – I was welcome to peruse the collection if I wanted to, to see what I found there, but in no way was I under any pressure to do so.

It was a foggy, dreamy morning when I decided I'd go there. The persimmon tree stood faint in the mist – I waved to it before losing sight of home from just twenty yards out. The owls weren't back from the hunt yet. It was very early morning. That day we were going to do gravity at school, and we were supposed to bring an apple with us. I thought it sounded interesting but if the past was anything to go by the science of it would be poorly explained.

I was aware as I walked towards the pond, in the periphery of my vision, of a little group of neighborhood Chrank kids playing at the edge of the woods, throwing their school bags around and being obstreperous. We often waited for the bus together. I didn't have a lot in common with them but we were all pretty friendly. Though this morning I was disappointed to see them – I thought I'd gotten there early enough to have beaten everyone else.

I tried to make my way surreptitiously to the pond. Which didn't look very inviting, after all: cold and mud-brown that morning, the figure nowhere in sight. The reflection of a single cloud skidding across its surface like the smear of a bug across a car's just-cleaned windshield.

Then one of them saw me, and asked where I was going.

Nowhere, I said.

He repeated the question. Chranks, you know: they know when you're most trying to avoid them and that's exactly when they come to haunt you.

The other Chrank kids became interested and approached us, gabbling. They understood quickly that the object was the pond, and they all wanted to know what I thought was in it. I wouldn't tell them. I said it was nothing. I said there wasn't anything in the pond but they refused to believe me. One of them saw the ambition in my eyes and guessed that there was something at the bottom that I wanted to look at. *Tell us*, they kept insisting. *Tell us what's there.*

I didn't want to. I refused to let anyone else in on my secret — honestly it wouldn't have mattered if they'd been some other kind of kid, I wouldn't have wanted them to come with me either. *I* was the one who had been talking to the figure. I was the one who knew about those books.

We were running out of time. I felt stupid for choosing the morning to do it. My logic had been that the light would be best then, but I realized too late that underwater the light's opposite anyway so probably midnight would have been as good a time as any for the trip. I was feeling so foolish now. I wanted them gone. These Chrank children, slowly surrounding me, chattering like squirrels, spoiling my plan.

In a few minutes they had me pinned to the ground. One of them, the one who'd spotted me in the beginning, was in charge of questioning. The others made sure my limbs were secure, that I had no way of moving. I wasn't frightened, only angry – angry because I refused to let them have my secret, and I felt stupid and humiliated to have to go to these lengths to prove it.

The leader, the smart one, leaned closer and closer to my face, asking me always what was at the base of the pond. I closed my eyes to try to ignore him but when his face got very close to mine I felt I could see him anyway so I might as well open them. It is too difficult to have another animal so close to you and not open your eyes to try to see what they're up to.

He won in that instant. When I opened my eyes he read what was written there.

'It's a library!' he told his Chrank buddies with triumph. He told them to release me. At the same time we all heard the sound of the schoolbus approaching.

The Chranks were confused and stood waiting for a cue from their leader. Their leader stood in an ambiguous position: half-facing myself and the other Chrank kids, half-facing the dark lure of the pond.

Many of them were still pinning me down, absentmindedly, as the yellow bus drew up. I wanted to shout with alarm. The owls flew overhead. They noticed my predicament in spite of their sleepiness, and they might have tried in some way to rescue me had it proved necessary. But the leader shouted just then, as if it were a battle-cry, *'Let's go!'* to all of the other Chrank children. So, with mixed expressions of faith and doubt, they followed their leader to the bottom of the pond.

The bus honked. I stood up. My heart was beating fast, and I had twigs in my hair. The bus honked again and I ran to catch it, never before so grateful for its cheerful yellow presence.

I got in and sat at the back, staring out of the window as the bus rumbled away. I still had my apple and I gnawed at it in shock. I was safe now, certainly. But I watched the pond and I watched it sadly. They had all dived under. There was no ripple on the surface. The Chranks were down there, reading all the books meant for me.

I knew even though no one had told me that after that day the figure would be gone. I knew my own chance to see the library had irrevocably passed. I decided then that I would have to leave that place as soon as I could, move somewhere where the libraries were vaster and public and all didn't depend on the green-gray whims of a figure.

What I didn't know was whether the Chrank children would make it back to the surface. To tell you the truth, it didn't much matter to me whether they did or they didn't. Either way, I was sure, I'd never forgive them.

It is an emotional story for me still. It drains me just to remember it. I was thinking about it when I got on the bus to go home today. I felt determined at last to tell it to someone at work. I was tired of letting them think I was some unmotivated loon.

I was still thinking about it all when we reached my stop and I stepped off the bus. The story pulsed in my mind like the horns of a big band. I couldn't forget the lost opportunity of that long-ago morning which had changed – possibly forever – the chances for my intellectual development. Dispensing (literally) the written word was as close since then as I'd come.

It was probably this thought that caused my distraction as I walked away from the bus stop. It accounts for the fact that I missed noticing the puddle. An ugly, deep, blue-gray thing, waiting to trip me – full of the runoff from the passing by traffic. I fell for it, stupidly. Stumbled right in. Crumpled my nice outfit into mud, sludge and gravel.

Wouldn't you know it? You can guess, can't you? They know when you're thinking about them. One had gotten off the bus behind me, I guess, and was walking in my trail like some kind of acolyte.

So when I looked up from the puddle, it was into the face

of a Chrank – speaking in that fast, distinctive way of theirs, asking if he could help me. Sure enough, he sported a dark pencil moustache.

The advantage they take! The superiority they feel! He'd probably quietly steered me toward the puddle just to watch me fall into it.

I looked up at his lean, pale face. At the learned hand he extended. My life's campaign against this sort rose up to choke me.

My knees itched and bled, my heart started pounding. I listened for a comforting bus rumble but there was only cold silence.

I balanced myself, then pulled one muddy hand out of the water. You tell me – in that dark situation, what else could I do?

The Lady in the Desert

I've heard about these starvation diets you can go on, and I thought it sounded like a good idea. So I decided to move to the desert. No temptations, right? Just sand and sky, the occasional constellation after dark. Sounds relaxing.

I'm trying to lose ten pounds.

Everyone says it should be pretty easy. I mean, I'm not like Abigail, who really could afford to drop thirty or even forty before she'd feel comfortable tanning on the beach. Abigail shops at the Lady Bountiful store where they sell the bigger items. Says the saleswomen there are so friendly and nice. Don't make you feel awkward, tell you you look good. Hold your other-colored options while you pace back and forth in front of the mirror. Walking the walk, giving a twirl.

Then there's Barb. She's never looked the same since her

kids. Never lost that weight back. Still has great wads of dough on either hip, love-handles you can call them for a joke, or if anyone you love actually handles them – doesn't happen in my life, not any more, not since Tony – but we all know what they really are is fat, fat, fat.

I'd like to be thin, myself. Obviously I haven't got a big problem with my weight – I'm only trying to lose ten pounds – but I'd like to be just that bit thinner, so that people would take a look at me and say to themselves, 'Now how does she keep her shape like that?'

Serenity, would be my answer. That and maybe cutting out doughnuts completely and sticking strictly to skimmed milk and margarine. Otherwise it's a state of mind. *Serenity*. I'll smile when I say it. Serene-like. Confident.

That's after I get back from the desert. While I'm here I don't have to worry about ordinary day-to-day things like what percent fat in the milk or yogurt, because of course here there isn't anything like that at all. No refrigerators. No dairy. No health and international aisle, no frozen veg, no party and picnicware, no clingfilm.

Nothing, like I said, but sand and sky.

I took a walk my first day here. It would be easy to get lost, I knew, so I took a multipack of sugarless gum I'd brought with me and left the wrappers sticking up in the sand for signposts. They stood up like bright little flags from around the world, marking my path. I chewed a lot of sugarless before

I realized I could use the wrappers without actually opening up and chewing all the gum inside. I'm so stupid sometimes! And it makes sense to save some gum for later. What else am I going to have to distract me round about Day Seven of my diet?

It was a pleasant walk, though. Smooth and yellow-white, a dry smell in the air. I wouldn't have minded a little birdsong, maybe a tree or a building on the horizon to break it up a little, but otherwise it was enjoyable. A thin breeze whisked around my face every now and then, which was refreshing what with the heat here. I wore my sun visor for protection and a dab of sunblock on my nose – I hate that Rudolph effect when you forget.

The sand got in my tennis shoes and made it hard to walk, but I got my rhythm going after a while. It's like being on a ship. On our honeymoon we went on a cruise ship and it took me some time to get my 'sea-legs.' (I'll never forget it – sliding back and forth along the deck, holding onto Tony, both of us laughing. He wasn't any better at it than me; in fact he was the one who couldn't keep his food down, poor guy.) Here I guess you could say it took me a few minutes to get my 'sand-legs,' but I did develop the technique after a while. You've got to relax, let your foot go all loose and follow the shape of the sand dune. Be flexible. Just don't expect solid ground and you're fine.

That's the last time I'm going to mention our honeymoon.

So I walked along, planting my gum wrappers every so often, humming a tune from *South Pacific*, one of my favorites. I thought about Jean's daughter's wedding in a couple of weeks and wondered if she's really going to look OK in that dress. They've had quite a to-do about that dress, with Jean telling her – and I agreed – that the *one* thing a wedding dress has to be is long. And with her legs! But Nickie insists she's going to wear it. 'It's the in thing, Mom,' she said, which you can't argue with, apparently. I'll be curious to see the pictures. Jean hugging her daughter, trying to smile like it isn't killing her.

I also thought a little, on my walk, about whether I really feel like paying more taxes like they're always talking about. I say, show me some results! Where does the money go? I mean, what are we paying for exactly besides people's private jets and ski vacations, and is that what the government is all about? This somehow got me worrying about the situation in the Middle East. All this sand, I was bound to start thinking about it. Why can't people get along there, I'll never understand. What is their problem, and is it worth it to keep fighting about it? They say Armageddon's lurking there, though I don't know that I believe them. Made me hotter just to think about it.

In this way the time passed fast, and when I'd worked up a good sweat I decided to head back. They say it's good for your heart to get some kind of aerobic exercise every day, if possible. This walk definitely qualified. I was a little dizzy by

the end but I think that had more to do with the sun and some
of those uncomfortable thoughts than because I'd overstrained
myself. I'm basically in good shape. I only get out of breath
by the third floor, where I work.

Luckily I was smart enough to bring an umbrella with me
on this trip, so when I got back to home base I opened it up,
propped it in the sand and stretched out under it. The sun was
slipping in the sky; it was late afternoon. I was doing great, so
far: what with the walk and my thoughts and making sure I
could follow the gum wrappers back, I hadn't thought about
food more than a couple of times. Anyway, it was too hot to
have much of an appetite.

I'll tell you the truth, though. What I did have a big craving
for there, under the umbrella, in that late heat? Was a
milkshake. A milkshake would have gone down so perfect
then: a nice, creamy chocolate shake with a rich malty
aftertaste. A McDonald's milkshake, in fact. They make pretty
good ones, you might not realize it but it's true. It's the malt
I love.

If not that, I could have gone for a fruit smoothie, my
second choice. To be healthy. The kind brightly colored
Hawaiian-type girls sell in stands on the street to make you
feel virtuous. Strawberries, bananas, honey, coconut, ice and
milk – it can't be a whole lot less calories than a milkshake,
but I guess at least you get the fiber and the vitamins.

I had to settle for a swig from my canteen. What could I

do? It was a starvation diet. Rules are rules. Besides, there wasn't anything else available.

To make myself stop thinking about the milkshake I took a novel out of my bag. My mouth was full of these juices — juices of the hunger for strawberries, the hunger for that malt flavor, for the periodic crunch of the ice between your teeth that makes you shiver.

I lay down under the umbrella using the canteen for a pillow. I tried to focus on my book. It was about an airport. Something was happening in an airport, someone caught sight of someone else who was supposed to be on a different flight but instead was on a flight to one of those cities that always shows up in books like that, Dubai maybe or Nicosia. It was a thriller.

I read three pages before I fell into a thick, hot doze. I dreamt about daquiris. Kind of like a party we had on the ship that time, though that was years ago. Rum, ice, crushed fruit: the feeling that none of it would end. They do that to you, vacations. Make you forget what's real.

When I woke up, I couldn't even remember the names of any of the characters in the book, and I knew I'd have to read those first few pages again.

It didn't take me long to develop a routine. I find a routine makes the day manageable. Otherwise you're sliding all over the place wondering where to go. That's why I, unlike a lot of people I know, am pretty happy about my job. In fact, I was really beginning to miss some of the girls already and wonder what they were getting up to. Abigail, Barb, Jean. Even Ellen. Even *Nancy*.

I'm not saying I didn't need a vacation. People said it was time I took one, that I was looking tired. Looking like I'd been under a lot of stress, which I had. The things you go through after a loss, you know? I'll tell you what, though. I didn't tell anyone where I was going, or about the diet. The worst thing is when you tell people something like that and then break it. Everyone knows. The second you leave the room they say, 'I knew she'd never be able to stick with it. I've seen how much she enjoys her french fries.' This way, when I go back, there will just be the shock; the silence; the admiration. 'What happened to *you?*' they'll say. A little jealous, of course. A little disappointed. 'You look *terrific!*'

So this is how my routine goes. I don't have a watch, which makes it tricky, but I go by the temperature and how high the sun is, white-hot, in the colorless sky.

Dawn. Wake up. Stretch. Do half an hour (approx) of calisthenics.

Morning break. Gargle once with water, then spit. Generous helping of water that's kept pretty cool by the desert night. Take one megavitamin. (Hopefully that's not cheating.)

Morning. Dress. Take a sand bath. A little itchy at first, but I've gotten used to them. Tidy clothes, roll up sleeping bag;

139

it's good to stay disciplined. Spend a couple of hours on organizational matters – writing up next year's Christmas list, for example, or planning for my summer budget.

Lunch. Three sips *maximum* of diet cola. It's the one thing I allowed myself to bring. But I only brought one can, because I felt guilty about it, so I have to ration the supply.

High noon. When the ball of heat is directly overhead. Nap. Sometimes it takes me a minute, because the diet cola has jazzed me up (I should have gotten caffeine-free), but then the heat soaks through to me. I find the rest useful.

Early afternoon. Go for a walk. I've got the gum wrapper system down to perfection. Sing a couple of songs from *South Pacific* or *Guys and Dolls*, or occasionally *Oklahoma!* There are three walks I do: the one where you go over the gentle slope into the slightly cooler dip of gray sand; the straightforward, straight ahead walk where nothing much changes; and the one where I walk in the other direction completely, where eventually you see the faint outline of a clump of trees. An oasis. I call this one Mirage Mile, because I don't believe those trees really exist.

Afternoon. Temperature's a tad cooler. I read under the umbrella. I try to keep my attention on the thriller – that first guy is dead by now, I know that much – but I still keep losing the thread and forgetting the characters' names, so I often have to go back to re-read. Every now and then a thought of a turkey club, or even a salad bar salad with ranch-style dressing, wings across my mind and temporarily blots out the novel. And then there are thoughts of Tony, though I try to wipe those out before they even get there.

Evening. The sun is low in the sky. I'm beat. It's been a long day. Dinner is a slice of sugarless gum. The good thing about the multipack is it has different flavors. Sometimes just for fun I'll ask myself, 'So what'll it be tonight?' And I'll answer, lifting up my sunglasses as if to take a closer look at the menu, 'I think I'll have the strawberry.'

Dessert is water.

Last but not least – my nightcap. One brief shot of whisky. Again, maybe a stretching of the rules – but so worth it. It calms and relaxes me after everything I've done. Besides, the pounds are melting off me, I can tell. I don't have a scale, but you know how it is, you can just tell. Your heart feels lighter. Your ankles that bit more delicate.

The only problem with the nightcap, on a bad night, is it can make you a little melancholy. The kinds of things that creep up on you: people you miss. Things you wish you'd done. Age, and the fact that another baseball season is already almost upon us.

Night. Ink blue and cold. I'm feeling pretty sleepy by now. I change into my nightgown and settle down in my comfy sleeping bag. Say a quick prayer, maybe. Think about my friends at home, wonder how they're doing. Count the days till Jean's daughter's wedding and hope they haven't been fighting too much. Finally, just before sleep, my last delicious indulgence of the day.

I think about the chocolate cake I'll have when I make it out of here. Thick fudge-creamy icing. Coconut. Moist, deep brown, sweet. Smelling like paradise. Like the cake in that restaurant the night I first met Tony.

I've decided to extend the diet, and the trip. It's just going so well. I'm sure they'll understand at work. It's too bad I can't call them to tell them – there's no phone here, of course. They'll just have to manage without me.

The girls won't recognize me when I get back. 'How'd you *do* it?' they'll ask, astonished. 'What's your secret?' I won't let on how I did it. I'll smile mysteriously. I'll treat myself to one or two new outfits, and watch people noticing me with a whole different attitude.

I've been talking to Tony some about it at night – about how great it feels to be this much lighter. I think he's proud of me. Don't worry, I'm not going crazy! I know Tony's gone and everything. I'm not that confused. Still, I find it a comfort to have a little chat with him before I go to sleep. Jean's daughter's wedding has come and gone, so I don't have that to think about any more. I gave up on the novel. One of the guys died by being thrown in a swimming pool bound and gagged, before he had a chance to tell the other guy, the airport guy, where he'd stashed the document that exposed the true nature of the business. I lost interest at that point. Besides, who needs references to swimming pools? I live in the desert now, and have to get used to it.

Tony always was a quiet guy. It's not so hard, to get used to him not talking back. Frankly, I just find it a help having him here at all, keeping me company, spurring me on with his silent ways, boosting my confidence about how terrific I'm looking. 'Thin, huh?' I'll say to Tony in the afternoon, after I get back from my walk. The sky will sometimes seem to darken and I may nearly fall over. When I get my balance again I'm even more excited. 'It's hard to tell I'm the same person, isn't it?' I'll say, and he can't do anything but agree.

I have a great ambition for the end of the day today. It's something I always meant to do before I go. I'm going to take my day's walk today on Mirage Mile, and see, though I know by definition it's impossible, if I can make it all the way to the trees at the end.

Tony's agreed to come with me. He thinks it's a nutty plan, but finally he had to go along with it. It was that way with our honeymoon, too. He thought a cruise trip sounded awful – to tell you the truth, Tony always hated the water, which makes it such a terrible coincidence that he died how he did – but when he saw that I had my heart set on it, what could he do? Tony was always sweet to me that way. I told him about the pictures I'd seen of a jewel-blue sea being cut in half by a diamond-white ship, on which all the people were blond and thin and smiling. Tony said, 'We're not blond or thin but I guess we could smile,' and so he booked us the tickets. I want to tell him now, 'Hey, Tony, at least *I* am now, you know! At least *I'm* thin now!' And who knows what they do to you in heaven, maybe he is too.

So he's agreed to come along. I explained to him my marker system. I explained how you put the little wrappers in the ground like they were the flags of the united nations, as if this walk we would take might somehow ensure world peace. I didn't tell him about higher taxes or the question of Armageddon. I thought it would depress him. Besides, I don't think about that stuff so much myself any more. When you're happy with yourself, the way I am now I'm thin, you don't have to focus on other people's ills.

My mind's so clear now. I've long since finished the diet cola, so I don't have that around to pollute me. I abandoned the exercise regime, it seemed a waste of time. I've forgotten exactly what the work was I had to do on my desk before I left – which I figure by now someone else has picked up anyway. I think about Jean, and Abigail and Barb, but in my mind now they are blurred and yellow, wearing the weak smiles of the somewhat forlorn. *Be happy*, I wish I could tell them from across this great expanse of desert. Shed that weight! Feel good about yourself! When you do, little things like wedding dresses won't get to you at all! If I can reach this kind of contentment, girls, I'm positive that *you* can.

'Happy talkie talk and happy talk . . .' I prepare for my walk, singing from *South Pacific*. When Tony's not watching me, I allow myself to gaze out at the sheer bone-whiteness of the sand and imagine what I'll find if I reach the oasis. Great tall palm trees dripping sweet dates. A coconut spilling its creamy smooth milk. An orange grove, possibly, studded with that sweetest purest fruit that hot countries provide. And by the deep blue pond of the clear, cool water, Tony dangling his toes, sunning himself in his gray trunks, enjoying life, his baseball cap jutting out over his eyes. This time there will be no accident. This time we won't lose him to his heart's waterlogged failure. I look at him longingly in the oasis and walk towards him, my now tan lean arms outstretched, my thin body model-glamorous and graceful. I take an armful of the fruits around me and approach him, my dear Tony, the man I've loved since that first chocolate cake.

He smiles at me but also tilts his head like something is bugging him.

'Ah, ah, ah——' he says to me in a scolding voice. 'Rules are rules, hon!'

He winks at me as if to indulge me, then relieves my arms of all that fruit. He takes an orange and slowly starts to peel it, watching me watch him as the peels spiral to the ground.

I want to kiss him, the orange juice on his lips looks so

145

good. But Tony's a mirage, and I know if I kiss him he'll melt away. So I let him go ahead and eat his orange. I have to be happy to keep my distance. I sit over on the other side of the big blue pond, and wait for myself weightlessly, hushed, to evanesce.

Mars Needs Women!

—Though why, I can't imagine. We've got a bunch of them down here, and where has it gotten us? Muriel's not talking to Sheila because of that famous phone call; Irene has just run off with Sally's ex, so everyone's going to have to choose sides; and Wilma keeps bragging about her kids, in spite of the fact that she hasn't got any. The only really notable beacon in the gloom is Helen, who has just designed the first solar-powered airplane. But then Helen's always been an overachiever.

So I said I'd volunteer. I could do with the break, to tell you the truth.

It's been a slow period for me here. Ever since the Christmas party there hasn't been a lot to do, and of course the Christmas fiasco took some recovering from.

I'm not sure who originally had the idea. These kinds of schemes sometimes seem to condense in the atmosphere. Suddenly all you know is that a holiday is approaching and everyone has decided it's time to have a bash. We were ripe for the big one. It had been a while. The fervor had been storing up for months, a shared eagerness to put ourselves – to put *everything* – out on display.

First of all there was all that build-up and preparation. Weeks of beating egg whites, soaking fruits, chopping nuts, sorting the wheat from the chaff – one of my favorite tasks, that last one, because of the metaphorical possibilities in it. I kneaded dough like there was no tomorrow. Grew dizzy from brandy fumes and giddy with the stolen sweetness of candied cherries. Later we slaughtered a pig for the holiday – Janet held on to poor Elmer while Sally did the dirty deed – and some of the other girls cleaned and cured the thing so that ultimately I'd have some nice sausage meat for those tasty canapés I make. That was later, of course, on the very day of the party, because they're really not so good if you do them ahead to freeze.

Clothes – what a nightmare. Always so hard to know what you're going to wear to an event like that. Silk, lace, crinoline? Velour, velvet, velcro? Long or short? Overstated or under? Fashion conscious, or something that actually looks good on the body? Same question comes up with color – whether to go with that nameless yellow-blue-green shade that's all the rage this year, or whether to break away, go with mauve, maroon, sienna, burnt orange? A brightness that flatters, a richness that charms? And then another query – diamonds and rhinestones dotted about the face and figure, or one great gem strategically stashed for maximum effect, a peak location for envy, admiration, curiosity – even lust, a little? On this kind of occasion, these are the questions that trouble me.

In the end I thought I'd go with black. Head to toe. Keep it simple. Nothing too special. Two quiet earrings hidden by my hair. A muted shade of lipstick. A suggestion of blush. A smear of eyeshadow – on my sleeve, accidentally, because the container spilled, but I left it there to keep attention away from my eyes. I didn't want anyone to notice my eyes.

Decorations took about a week. We all helped. Muriel and Sheila trekked up hills and down, felling about fifteen pine trees. This was before the famous disastrous phone call, when they still worked pretty well together as a team. They trussed up the trees and hauled them in so some of the rest could get to work cutting them up in various dimensions depending on their use: firewood, Christmas ornament, a couple of decent planks for buffet tables and some good solid stakes on which to hang the streamers and welcome banners. One precious guy held back to be the Christmas tree itself – a big honor, though you can imagine the squabbling that went into deciding which one it should be.

The whole factory here gave over to making parts of

decorations. Normal work was put off for one whole week: production was suspended on miniskirts, bikinis, headscarves, and handbags; leggings, berets, sweatsuits, and tutus. All of that had to take a back seat while the seamstresses sewed their Christmas magic. Red and green tablecloths. Green and red napkins. Green sachets, pillows, doilies, coasters. Red carpets. Red seat-covers. Red oven mitts. A variety of cut-out shapes of a seasonal sort: reindeer, elves, candy canes and moons.

On the silver and gold end of things we had Irene working flat out. No one knew yet she was going to run off with Sally's ex — we were all still so innocent then of the way trusts can be shattered — and Irene did always have a way with metallicized surfaces. She has some very clever technique for shredding tinfoil into thin strips for tinsel. Everyone's tried for years to get her to give over her secret, but she won't let on. She's not a big sharer. There's also this neat thing she does with gold chocolate wrappers to produce a very pretty and unusual kind of streamer-chain — it takes your breath away when it's hanging along the wall and the light hits it just so.

And the rest of the team working just as hard picking berries and sprigs and pinecones and tufts of things, for the wreath upon wreath that were dutifully woven together. I popped a huge vat of popcorn so that a day or two before several of us could string popcorn and berries, a little trick that Wilma thought wouldn't be worth the effort until she saw how pretty the end effect was. White-cranberry, white-white cranberry, white-cranberry, white-white – beautiful.

Oh, the place was looking good. Was it ever. We'd decided to cordon off the whole meadow, then use the barn and the old schoolhouse for the food and drink and indoor festivities. That had been the plan. Then Helen came along, bless her heart – who'd have thought she'd have time to spare for something like a party, with all the important work she does! – and designed and oversaw the building of a giant yurt. You know those things. Hexidexigramigons or something – there's a scientific name for them, anyway. Round globe-like buildings that look like giant nightlights and are self-everything: you hardly need to heat or light them, they're so efficient. She made ours big enough for dancing and carousing, big enough for all the food tables. I told her ahead of time to take into consideration the fact that I was planning on making 150 sausage puffs *alone*. She got the idea. It was a mega-yurt.

But, I'll tell you, the night before I had an inkling something was going to go wrong. I talked to Sally about it on the phone, I was so worried. She was still washing all the pig's blood off her hands from the slaughter. It was hard to get out, apparently. I heard mellow splashes in the background as we talked. The occasional, 'Out, damn you!' – not addressed to me – though it's not like Sally to use bad language.

'Something's wrong,' I told her. 'I don't know what, but something is.'

153

'Not enough food?'

'Plenty of food.'

'Decorations won't be up in time?'

'They're starting at five tomorrow morning, a team of twenty. I think there's time.'

'Worried about your dress?'

'The dress is fine. Nothing special, but—'

'Out, goddammit!'

'What?'

'Stupid spot. Sorry. Nothing. So what do you think it is?'

'I don't know. A premonition.'

'Some sort of disaster?'

'Yes.'

'Unnatural or natural? Or supernatural?'

'I don't know. Natural, maybe. Natural? Yes. A fire. Thunder and lightning. An earthquake, possibly, on an outside chance.'

'We'll be careful. We'll store some flashlights and a bucket of water somewhere just in case. A radio with fresh batteries. It's always good to listen to premonitions. They can speak the truth.'

In the end, of course, the disaster was all too predictable. I didn't even have time to notice it, myself, until lateish in the evening. I was so busy cooking, folding, wrapping, spearing, stuffing little niblets, preparing gleaming trays of food. Dabbing a bit of butter on the top here, garnishing with a sprig of parsley and a lemon wedge there. People kept telling me,

'Take a break! Take a break!' but it was long after sundown before I finally did. That's what happens when you're making food on that scale, you get on a roll and you just have to keep going. Keep your head down and keep at it for the sake of the others. By the time I finally stopped and looked around me the problem, the disaster, was screechingly clear.

No one had come.

No one, that is, besides all of us. *We* were all there. The gals from the factory, Sally and Irene (without the ex, thank God), Muriel, Sheila, Janet, myself, the girls from the rodeo, the pig-keepers, the gardeners, that lady who lives in the watchtower, Gretchen the hermit who keeps the unfriendly cat. Helen even took an hour off from work to stop by, which was awfully sweet of her. Yes, we were all there. But where was everybody else?

It was a crushing blow. You know how that is. All that effort and planning, all that excitement. The mad adrenaline skidding through your veins as the hours of the day wear on, as you get closer and closer to the time the festivities begin. The anticipation that doesn't even have an object finally but just crouches colorful and shapeless in your mind, of what might happen later in the night. The personalities, the songs, the drunken brushings up against one another. The controversies. The triumphs. All of it hides in your imagination waiting to happen and blurs the many minutes and hours of preparation. Until something clicks over and your internal clock starts to alarm. Then, somewhere towards the close of that long day, though you're in the middle of cooking, you rush out for a few minutes and lock yourself in a room to get out of your frumpy day-clothes and into that dress. You pull the dress on and even if it is only middle-length and nothing too special you start to feel thrilled. You start to feel glamorous. In a small reflecting square you watch yourself highlight the excitement on your face with a dab here, a pat there, a rubbing of a little cream or powder in a few sensible spots so that your face begins to emerge a special face, a face worth looking at. With the stockings and pumps on you know you're ready to pull and push and fondle the hair into the right shape, natural but sculpted, thick but not bushy, shiny but not oily, smelling fresh like fruits, like some desert fruits. When you return to the cooking tasks you are a different person, and though you cover yourself with something so you won't get spilled on you can't cover over the essential fact that you're ready for the party now, that you're on, you're waiting, come on, bleep!, *go*.

Only to find. Only to find a room full of familiar faces, picking at your sausage puffs edgily and pointing out each other's shortcomings. Playing cards at a corner table. The odd desultory waltz to the falling flat music.

We didn't designate an inviter. That was our mistake. We just never singled out someone to put together a guest list. One of those typical things – everyone thought someone else was doing it. There wasn't even anyone to blame. Though in that kind of environment people start to get suspicious. Sally narrowed her eyes at Irene as if she might somehow be behind it all, and for nefarious reasons; Muriel and Sheila introduced each other's names as possible architects of the foul-up, thus providing an augur of the bad things to come.

Myself, I wasn't in the mood to blame. I was too exhausted, too disappointed; too depressed, in fact, to think it important to find a culprit. I didn't say anything. I sat in a corner in my dress sampling some canapés (I hadn't eaten anything all day, I'd been too excited) and absorbing the occasional compliment about my skills in the kitchen. I told one of the factory girls how beautiful the decorations were. I hung a gold star on the tree – everyone was supposed to put one decoration on it, that was part of the party program. I listened to the women around me talking and I watched the first disintegration of so many fine friendships. A few harsh words were exchanged. The alcohol made some folks rowdy. People said things they might later regret. The ground was paved – well, you'd be able to see this in retrospect – for that famous phone call, for the terrible betrayal of one woman by another, a common event in the scheme of things, I know, but not something any of us had yet come to expect.

Plus there was so much to clean up, afterwards.

I won't bother listing who stayed behind to help and who just went home to bed, leaving it for everyone else. There's really no point in naming names. Some people understand the collective effort required in these things and some people don't. Some people nurture a forgetful streak for just that moment. (You know the type.) But it's not important now. Suffice it to say the core group of us didn't get to sleep that night till nearly dawn.

Even so I didn't sleep much. I couldn't. Too keyed up still. Also it's my job in the mornings to feed the chickens, and party or no party, catastrophe or no catastrophe, the chickens were going to be hungry. They'd want to be fed. So I was up just after the roosters, same as usual.

'You're going to get a good breakfast this morning, sweethearts,' I told them, lugging over my pail of party scraps, before I realized with embarrassment that Helen was hanging around by the coop and probably heard me.

I was surprised to see her. She spends a lot of time indoors, of course, working on her big ideas. When I asked what she was doing there, though, she said sometimes she just liked to listen to the sounds the chickens made, that she found it soothing. Then, in the broad daylight we were standing in, she noticed, as she was bound to, that there was something wrong with my eyes. Delicately – she is a sensitive soul, is Helen – she asked me what was wrong with them.

I had to tell her.

'I've been looking up at Mars,' I confessed to her. 'I'm thinking of going there.'

She asked me why.

I shrugged. 'They need women,' I said simply. 'I don't know, I figured it would be a change of pace.'

I told her what I knew about life up there, which wasn't a lot – impressions and rumors more than hard facts. They have a lot of meetings there, apparently. People play squash and racquetball. They read the papers. There's quite a lot of train travel: some, I've heard, take two or three trips *every day*.

Helen concurred with all this. Of course she'd know something about it, she's the one with the brains around here. She told me a few other items she'd gathered over the past few years. That on Mars they had microwaves. It's some way of heating food instantly – you can bake a potato in a matter of seconds, reheat coffee in the blink of an eye. In addition they have the convenience of toaster ovens and high-speed blenders. Also nuclear bombs, though I wasn't clear how they'd be useful. And they were just now developing the technology to make an alarm clock that could read your mind and go off exactly when you wanted it to – *by playing whatever music you were in the mood for*.

'Helen, that's terrific,' I told her. 'Don't you want to come?'

But she didn't want to, for some reason. She said she'd rather stay here with everyone else.

'We'll miss you,' she told me. So sweet of her! I honestly wouldn't have thought she'd have time to notice.

'Thanks, Helen,' I said, tilting my face unstoppably up, to try to get a glimpse of the place I might be going. But Helen covered my brow with her hand to prevent me from looking. She was keeping off the rays. She made a quiet tsking sound like the cluck of a chicken, and said she didn't want to see me do any more damage to my pretty green eyes.